Fwl or Fool?
Part one

By T. J. Thomas

Contents

CARWEN

Fwl approached Carwen Castle.

Truly magical.

Every time he visited Carwen, he was struck by its grandeur and magnificence. The castle perched on huge, billowing clouds, overlooking the lush green land below. The tall, imposing walls of smooth white stone glowed in the morning light.

Fwl entered the castle through a massive arched doorway and found himself in the bustling foyer. The air was filled with chatter and laughter. Gods of all kinds milled about, coming and going from various rooms. The corridors of the castle seemed to stretch on forever.

For the hundredth time that day, he looked at the card he was clutching.

Fwl, a god of Melyn,
You are required to attend a meeting at
Carwen.
Room 101 at 11 a.m.

Fwl smiled at a passer-by and hesitantly approached the information desk. The young lady sitting behind it smiled as he approached.

'Good morning,' she said.

'Good morning, I have a meeting in Room 101, at 11 o'clock.'

She gestured to the right. 'Please take a seat.' Fwl walked to where she had indicated and sat on the edge of a chair. *A remarkable place*, he mused. It was the official meeting place of all the gods of Hiraeth, and Fwl loved every inch of it.

Fwl took a seat next to a young man. The young man was sitting in the chair with his back straight, his feet planted firmly on the ground. His hands were clasped tightly in his lap.

'Hello, my name is Fwl.' He said holding out his hand. 'Lovely to meet you.'

'Oh hello.' He said taking Fwl's hand. 'My name is Eric.' He leaned in close and said. 'It's my first day.'

'How wonderful!' Fwl said. 'You are going to love it here.'

'I'm not sure what all of this is about actually. I was just told to come here.' Eric said.

'I can explain some of it if you'd like?'

'Yes, please. If you don't mind.'

'The people of Hiraeth are each designated a god. That would be us.' He nudged Eric and smiled. 'Not that the people know this; they are not religious in any way, shape or form. They are blissfully unaware of the system of gods. Imagine a hierarchy.' Fwl said holding up his arms, making a shape of a pyramid. 'At the bottom would be the gods of Gwyn. They are used as, let's say, *watchers*, sent by other gods to watch the people and gather information. They are like spies, so to speak.' He leaned into Eric and whispered. 'Being a god of Gwyn is quite embarrassing. It's a well-known fact among the gods that if you're in the Gwyns, you've either made a gigantic mistake as a god or are generally rubbish at your job. All the other gods avoid making eye contact with the Gwyns; they just pretend they're not there, so as not to jinx their own place in the hierarchy.'

Fwl slapped his hands on his lap. 'Let's see, ah yes, a step up from the Gwyns are the gods of Melyn. If you meet a god of Melyn give them all the help they need because they are just one more mistake from being demoted to a god of Gwyn … and they'll be losing sleep over it. The next level up from the gods of Melyn are the gods of Glas. Then the gods of Du, who are the elite. All other gods praise them and strive to be like them. They are perfect in everything they do.'

Fwl glanced at Eric unsure if he was following. He continued. 'At the very top of the pyramid are the gods of Popeth. They are the decision-makers, the managers if you will. The gods of Popeth are the ones that assign each god to one or more people from Hiraeth. There are many gods – hundreds – each with their own ward or wards to inspire and guide. Did that help?' Fwl asked.

Eric frowned, 'Um I think so. That's a lot to take in.'

'You'll get used to it. Don't you worry.' He patted Eric's leg.

As far as Fwl was concerned, this was the best job in the world.

'Fwl?' the woman behind the desk called.

'Yes!' He jumped up and rushed to the desk.

'You'll be having the meeting on the 5th floor.'

'Thank you very much.'

He turned to Eric. 'It was lovely meeting you.'

Fwl closed his eyes for a second, then he appeared on the 5th floor. He'd never been that high up in Carwen before. The corridors on this floor were lined with vibrantly coloured tapestries. He walked down the corridors and came across the first room. '97'. Room 101 should be a little further down. As he walked, he caught a glimpse of various rooms, each one as breath-taking as the next. Some were full of gold and priceless artefacts, others were filled with books as far as the eye could see.

'How wonderful,' he said out loud.

'Excuse me, kind sir,' Fwl asked a passer-by. 'Could you tell me where Room 101 is?'

The man pointed. 'Three doors down.' As Fwl walked away, the man added, 'Good luck.'

Fwl stopped in his tracks and stared at the retreating figure.

'Oh, um, thank you.' His stomach fluttered. Good luck? Why would he need good luck?

He walked down the corridor and came across a guard standing outside Room 101.

The guard stood with his shoulders back and chest out. His uniform was neatly pressed. His face looked stern as if he was constantly scanning his surroundings for potential threats.

'You can't come in here,' the guard barked.

'But,' Fwl stammered, 'I have an appointment.'

The guard puffed out his chest. 'You can't come in.'

'But I have a card.' Fwl held up his appointment card.

'A card?'

'Yes, I have a meeting at 11, see?' He jabbed at the card.

The guard snatched it from Fwl and peered at it.

'Why didn't you say so?'

'I did.'

'Right, right,' said the security guard dismissively. 'I'll go and let him know you're here.' He turned and walked down the corridor, then stopped and looked back over his shoulder. 'Your name is 'fool'?'

'Yes, but it's spelt F-W-L.' he said, 'Let who know I'm here?'

'Wait here,' barked the guard.

Every time someone learnt his name, they all had the same confused look and the same questions. 'Your name is 'fool'?' or 'Who the hell named you 'fool'?' Little did they know his name had come first. Fwl had always loved his name. It was a strong name for a god. People would respect it. But then Sebastian ruined it with his little joke.

Sebastian is a god of Glas. He had been guiding one of his wards, Jeff, one day. Jeff and his son, David, had an accident in a horse and cart, when one of the wheels had bounced off. While David tried to put the wheel back on, he snapped the prongs and broke it.

'Look at what you've done!' screamed Jeff.

'You're an absolute … um, an absolute …' he stuttered.

Sebastian leaned in and whispered in Jeff's ear, 'An absolute Fwl.'

'You're an absolute fool!' screamed Jeff.

David looked shocked and slightly confused. 'What's a fool? What does that even mean?'

'It means you're an idiot,' he said and clipped his son's head with his hand. The term 'fool' was born, and now everyone was using it as some sort of insult.

Sebastian spent weeks telling that story over and over to every god. Even now, when he sees Fwl, he recounts it and holds his belly in laughter.

Fwl brushed down his yellow suit while he waited; he always liked to look smart. All the gods wore suits, and each level of the pyramid had its own colour. The gods of Gwyn had white suits. Those of Melyn had yellow, Glas blue, and the gods of Du wore black. Fwl didn't know what colour the gods of Popeth wore – he'd never met any of them – but he suspected it would be a magnificent red. He often wondered why all the levels had colours, and had asked some gods why, but even they couldn't answer.

At that moment, Fwl was a god of Melyn. He was once a god of Glas. Unfortunately, he had made a mistake some years earlier and was demoted a level, but he was lucky not to be a Gwyn. He shuddered at the thought. He hadn't made a mistake since; he'd kept his head down and got on with his work, as he'd learnt in training.

He combed his fingers through his black wavy hair, then saw a full-length mirror down the corridor. He quickly ran to it and adjusted his tie.

'I told you to wait over there!' the guard's voice rang through the corridor.

Fwl jumped and rushed back to his original spot.

'Sorry, I just wanted to make sure everything was in place.' He patted down his hair, thinking it might have moved when he ran.

The security guard looked at him with an odd expression, then opened a door and said, 'Wait in here.'

'Right, okay, thank you.' Fwl walked through the doorway then looked back. 'You don't happen to know why I'm here?'

'How would I know?' The security guard slammed the door.

Fwl looked around the room. It was large and dark. Black tapestries covering the white stone walls. The only place on the wall that didn't have a tapestry was the small window that let in weak, grey light.

In the centre of the room was an impressive table handcrafted from thick oak. Fwl approached it for a closer inspection. The legs had been carved into thousands of people reaching up their arms. He took a step back and saw the people appeared to be holding up the tabletop.

'Amazing,' he said out loud.

He turned to face the enormous fireplace that looked like it hadn't been used for a long time. Above it hung a tapestry bearing the image of a powerful god.

It was Owain! This was Owain's office! Fwl's hands began to sweat. Why would Owain want to see him?

His brain started to work overtime and his thoughts overlapped. He squeezed his eyes shut to try and organise the chaos in his overthinking mind.

Fwl had only met Owain once. When he was demoted to Melyn status, if it wasn't for the god of Du, he was sure he would have been further demoted to the Gwyns.

What did I do to be summoned here? I've been in Oldport for the past two days, but I didn't do anything!

He had stood in the corner of that tavern and just listened, most certainly not interacting with anyone. He had followed his training. He wasn't seen by anyone. He definitely didn't leave anyth—

He gasped and slapped his hand over his mouth, then frantically patted himself down.

I left it there! Panic started to take hold.

His hand stopped at the pocket on his left leg. *Thank goodness*, he said to himself, as he pulled out a piece of paper with his instructions on it.

He let out a loud sigh of relief.

Thrusting the paper back into his pocket, he told himself he definitely hadn't done anything wrong. He was not reassured by his own thoughts.

He looked around again. The room was meant to intimidate him, and it was working.

Fwl heard voices outside the office.

'Is he in there?' said one voice.

'Yes, sir!' shouted the guard.

The door flung open and in swooped Owain in his black suit. He looked so powerful and magical. His presence commanded attention. His walk alone showed confidence and strength. His hair was black and unmoving, sitting perfectly. Owain's piercing eyes shot at Fwl. That look made Fwl's heart beat faster.

Owain walked past Fwl and sat at the table. The guard whipped the door shut, sending a wave of panic through Fwl's chest.

'Please sit, Fwl,' Owain said, gesturing with his hand to the seat opposite him.

Fwl rushed to the table and eagerly sat down. He faced Owain with a large smile.

'Thank you for coming.'

'I didn't know the card was from you, Owain,' said Fwl. 'I haven't seen you since, well …'

Owain raised his hand. 'Yes, it's been a while. He lowered his hand. 'That's why I've asked you to come today.' Owain's tone was serious as he took a deep breath. 'She's causing problems.'

Fwl's face dropped and he blushed at the unexpected words. *Mavis.* His greatest mistake. He loved her, of course, like the other gods love their wards, but she'd been challenging for years.

This meeting was not going to end well.

'Um, well, she's always tried to cause problems,' he said, waving his hand dismissively. 'I wouldn't worry; no one believes her. They say she's crazy.'

Owain stared at Fwl for several seconds. Fwl shifted in his seat.

The god of Du finally broke the silence. 'She's made a deal with the Dewin.'

Fwl shot up from his chair. 'She can't have!' he shouted. 'The Dewin are evil. They use their magic for dark, wicked reasons;

sometimes just for fun. How does she know about them?'

'Keep your voice down, Fwl,' Owain said calmly. 'Sit down.'

Fwl sank into his seat.

'I was told yesterday about the situation, by a Popeth,' Owain said.

Fwl shot to his feet again. 'A Popeth!'

A Popeth knows? A Popeth spoke to Owain about it! I'm going to be exiled or killed. Or worse I'm going to be demoted into a Gwyn!

'Fwl!'

'Sorry,' whispered Fwl and eased back into the chair.

A warmth crept through him and he started to sweat. He pulled at his collar and glanced at the fireplace to see if it had magically come to life without him noticing. Nope, still cold.

'Apparently, they approached her; she didn't go looking for them. They have a wicked sense of humour. They've always known about us, but using Mavis to make it public may compromise our system.' Owain took a deep breath. 'You need to fix it. Now the Dewin are involved, it's serious. You need to convince her to stop telling people about us.'

'I don't know how to,' Fwl said, panic rising to his throat. Leaning forward, he whispered, 'Honestly, if I knew how to fix it, I would have done it sixty-two years ago.'

'Fwl.' Owain rested his elbows on the table and clasped his hands together. 'You must go to her and convince her to stop.'

'I have spoken to her about it, Owain,' Fwl urged. 'She won't listen. She calls me the devil's messenger and tries to curse me.'

'She doesn't have the ability to curse you, Fwl.'

'That doesn't stop her from trying,' said Fwl, waving his hand. 'Every time she tries, she fails and ends up throwing things at me.'

'And those things go through you?'

'Well, yes, but it still hurts. Maybe not physically, but, you know.' He paused. 'It hurts my feelings. She says things to me. Hurtful things.' Fwl turned his head slightly so Owain wouldn't see his emotion.

'What do you mean?'

'She calls me names.'

Fwl felt that Owain wasn't taking this as seriously as he should. He leaned forward again and whispered, 'She has become a mean old lady!'

'Have you been doing your job? Guiding her? Inspiring her?'

'I try, but she doesn't listen. It's impossible to guide her when she doesn't pay any attention to me.'

Owain shook his head slightly. Fwl wasn't sure if it was because of the name-calling or because he didn't care.

'Fwl, you are being tasked with stopping her.' Owain opened a drawer under the table and extracted a piece of paper. 'Here are your instructions,' he said, pushing the paper towards Fwl.

Fwl stared at the sheet on the table between them. Should he pick it up or refuse the task? He didn't want to know what the instructions were. If he failed to convince Mavis, what would they instruct him to do? He knew she wouldn't listen.

'Couldn't you or another Du take up the task?' he said suggestively. 'She might listen to you.'

'How?' Owain said. 'She can't see us or hear us, only you!'

Fwl placed his hands in his lap and looked at them.

21

Owain sighed. 'I'm sorry, Fwl, but this has been a stressful time for me,' he said softly. 'The Popeth are angry that it has come to this. They're angry I got involved all those years ago, and they want her stopped. Please, take the task.'

Fwl looked up from his hands and took a deep breath. 'Do you or the Popeth have any suggestions on how to stop her?'

Owain pointed at the paper on the table. 'Your instructions are there. Please read them carefully.'

Both gods stared at each other for a second, then Fwl reached forward.

He held the paper for a moment, staring ahead, then read the instructions. 'Oh, Owain, please, I can't do this!'

'I'm sorry, Fwl, you have no choice. The Popeth believe that the Dewin will act in fourteen days.'

Owain stood and walked to the window. Looking out, he said, 'It will take a lot of convincing for her to change her mind.' He took a deep breath. 'They are allowing you thirteen days.' He turned back Fwl. 'If you fail, you must carry out your instructions.' He pointed at the paper in Fwl's trembling hand.

'There's something else,' Owain added. His expression became soft, almost pitiful. 'The Popeth want you to spend the thirteen days with her – every single minute. Even when she sleeps, you will not leave her. You will not be allowed to return to Carwen until the job is done. Do you understand?'

'Yes.'

'Can you sense where she is now?'

Fwl closed his eyes. 'She's in the north of Hiraeth, in Nabeth.'

'Go to her straight away and don't leave her side. It's very important that you carry this through.'

Fwl's stomach tumbled at the prospect of his quest. 'May I ask …' he started and cleared his throat. 'What was the price she paid?

'Her soul,' replied Owain.

'What a fool I am,' said Fwl miserably.

He turned to look at Owain, hoping he would disagree, but he just silently stared back at him.

Fwl closed his eyes and appeared in Nabeth. He stood at the end of the road, watching Mavis for a while.

'It's all a game!' she shouted.

She had a round figure with chubby cheeks. Each time Fwl saw her, she was wearing similar clothes – brown, beige, sometimes grey, and almost always threadbare.

Poor Mavis, she's like this because of me.

She'd had all those years and done nothing with them. She'd never had a job or even much of an education. She'd never married or had children. Never had any friends. And she was always angry, well, when Fwl was around.

'It's all just a game!'

Fwl stepped closer and saw that she had a sheet wrapped around her shoulders and knotted around her neck … like a makeshift cape. Written on the back were the words, *It's all a game.*

Fwl sighed.

He had tried to talk to her so many times; to try and convince her to live her life and enjoy the little time she had on Earth, but she would never listen to him.

Fwl crossed the road and walked to where Mavis stood at the corner of Market Street.

'It's all a game,' she shouted again.

Passers-by were avoiding eye contact and walking around her as if an invisible shield surrounded her and pushed them away. The closer she tried to get to them, the further they were pushed.

'I know the truth!' she screamed. 'I've seen it with my own eyes!'

The people of Nabeth knew she was a crazy old woman; that's what they called her, anyway.

'The crazy old lady is out again,' they would say.

'Hello, Mavis.'

Mavis snapped around so fast, Fwl swore she was facing that direction the whole time. She raised her hand and stretched out a chubby finger.

'There he is!' She pointed and screamed towards him. 'There's my proof!'

'Mavis, please,' said Fwl, raising both hands to try and calm her. 'Shhh,' he said in a light tone. 'Please, stop screaming. You know they can't see me.'

Mavis frantically looked around for witnesses. 'There he is!' she screamed, turning back at Fwl. 'Look!' Her outstretched arm was shaking at him. She raced up to a group of people, but the invisible shield pushed them further away.

Mavis bent to pick up a handful of stones and started throwing them at Fwl.

He raised his arms to protect his head, then, remembering the stones couldn't hit him, he lowered them, straightened his tie and brushed down his suit.

He cleared his throat loudly. 'Mavis.'

Stones were still hurtling through him and landing on the ground behind him.

Ignoring his hurt feelings, he said, 'I've been told that you've made a deal with the Dewin.'

'Be gone! Be gone, you messenger from the devil! I will not be a part of your game,' she screamed, just as a stone whirled through his nose and hit the ground.

Mavis turned back to look at the people in the street. No one had taken any notice. She let out a sigh.

'Mavis, I need to speak with you.' Fwl took a deep breath. 'I need you to stop this nonsense with the Dewin. You know as well as I do that it won't end well for you.'

Mavis huffed, hitched up her skirt and marched away.

'You know I can't allow you to get the Dewin involved. Mavis? Are you listening to me?'

She picked up speed, and Fwl quickened his stride to keep up with her.

'I am begging you to stop this!' he pleaded.

Mavis stopped dead and turned to him, her face puffy and red.

'You listen here,' she growled, taking a step closer and raising her hand to point at him. 'I will not have my life played out by someone else. I have told you a hundred times, I will not be controlled by you, and neither should anyone else.'

'It's not like that, Mavis. I've told *you* this before. We are *not* playing games with your life,' he said, trying to sound reassuring.

'Well, that's what I heard!'

He held up his hands defensively. 'That's not what I told you. We guide people to make decisions ... the right decisions.' He smiled weakly.

'Yes, control our thoughts!' she snapped. 'And the stronger gods have the most powerful people under their control, and they can do what they want!'

Fwl couldn't argue with that. 'I *don't* control you, Mavis.'

'I know,' she sneered, 'because I won't *let* you.' She leaned in closer to his face, so much so that he had to lean his head back. For a second, he was worried his neck would snap. Of course, he could have stayed still but her head would have gone through his, which would have been uncomfortable for both of them. He was just being polite.

Mavis pulled away and continued her march down the street.

'That's not how it works,' he said as he tried to catch up. 'I don't guide you because …' What were the right words? Words that wouldn't push her over the edge, well, any more than she already was.

'It's not that you won't *let* me. It's more that I *can't* guide you.'

He'd had this conversation with her before and it had ended with her trying to set him on fire. She always tried to hurt him physically. She couldn't, of course, but she never gave up trying.

'And what about everyone else? You control them!' she snapped, breathing heavily and slowing her pace a little.

'I don't control them; I've told you this,' he said calmly. 'I guide them. I help them make good choices. Let's stop and talk for a moment.'

Her breathing was laboured. 'Leave me be, you messenger from the devil.'

'Where are you going?'

Mavis picked up speed and turned down Murray Street. Fwl noticed the houses were less well kept there. The bushes and trees were overgrown, the cobbles were broken up as if someone had taken a sledgehammer to them. The houses were in need of repair. The further they walked down Murray Street, the worse it got. All the houses seemed to merge into one big building ... an ugly one. The people were sitting in the street, looking almost zombie-like.

Fwl glanced around nervously. 'Why are you going down here?'

Mavis carried on walking.

'This is not a good place to be walking,' he said, looking around, then gasped and stopped. 'Mavis, the godless live here!'

The godless were the ones that the gods gave up on. No matter how many times they tried, they could not get through to these types. The job of the gods was to help,

29

motivate and encourage, but some people couldn't be helped. Fwl had imagined there weren't many godless people, but the more he looked around, the more he realised there were many of them.

'Mavis!' he shouted. 'Why are you here?'

She stopped and turned. 'If you must know, I live here.'

'HOW DARE YOU! YOU ARE NOT GODLESS!' Outrage burned in him.

Mavis rolled her eyes at him and walked away.

He dashed after her. 'I'm sorry, I didn't mean to shout, but you are *not* godless.'

She didn't look back.

'I don't understand,' he said, struggling to keep up. 'I've always provided for you. I arranged for food to be brought to you regularly and for Mrs Davies to allow you to spend the rest of your days in her house,' he said, utterly confused as to why she was living in this awful place.

'She's dead,' Mavis said bluntly.

How had Fwl missed that? 'When did she pass away?'

'About three months ago,' she snapped.

'And you've been living here ever since?'

'No, I only just moved here,' she said. 'I was living in a barn with cows, but the owner threatened me with his shotgun.'

He had failed her.

No wonder she thought of herself as godless. No wonder she was there amongst those heathens. Fwl shot a sideways glance at a man who seemed to be sleeping, coughing and dribbling at the same time. He picked up his pace to catch up with his ward.

'Mavis, plea—'

'Stop talking, you fool,' she snapped. He hated it when she called him that. They both knew she wasn't calling him by his name.

Mavis turned right, followed a path and pushed open a wooden door. Fwl walked in after her. The wooden door led into a single room. There was a sink and a cupboard, and a pile of blankets in a corner in place of a bed. The walls were black with damp. Fwl felt sick. He had failed her. Completely.

Mavis picked up a large bag on top of the pile of blankets and walked out.

'Mavis!'

She didn't answer, and he took one more look around the room. His stomach lurched.

Fwl rushed after her. 'How long were you living there?'

'About a month,' she said. 'Do you still think I'm not godless?' She laughed at him.

Her heavy breathing worried Fwl, and she wasn't showing any signs of slowing.

'Where are we going?'

'I don't know where you're going, but I'm going south.'

'Wait, wait, wait,' he said, waving his arms and jumping in front of her.

She walked straight through him, but he carried on talking.

'I can't allow you to carry on like this, Mavis. I've watched you go crazy for too many years. I'm putting my foot down.'

She turned to him. 'Do you think you can stop me? After all these years, you've never been able to stop me doing anything.'

Fwl cleared his throat. 'You are my ward, Mavis. I won't allow you to see the Dewin.'

Mavis started to laugh. It was a small light laugh that turned into a loud barking cackle.

It sent shivers up Fwl's spine. 'Stop laughing.'

Mavis walked to the end of the street and turned left. Fwl watched her go. He could still hear her laughing when she was out of sight. He had always known her life wouldn't be like everyone else's; that was why he had tried to put things in place for her to live comfortably.

He dropped his head and followed her slowly.

SEREN

'Good morning, Fred,' Seren called from the side door of the cottage.

Fred stood as still as a tree, looking in the opposite direction.

Seren called out to Fred every morning, but he never acknowledged her. He was always busy protecting his field.

This field was his. The other sheep could have the field next door; this one was his.

Seren worried about Fred. He always had that look about him, like he was angry. He wouldn't share the field with any of the other animals. She knew this because she'd tried countless times. She'd even tried pushing him in with the others but he'd just dug his cloven hooves into the dirt. She had four other sheep and they wouldn't go anywhere near Fred. He was large for a sheep, with longer legs than most. His wool was a mixture of black and white, but mostly black.

Seren sighed and walked back into the cottage.

'IT WALKS IN THROUGH THE DOOR!'

This greeting was from her late husband's aderyn, Birdy.

An aderyn is a talking bird. Not only does it talk, but it repeats what it sees. They don't always do this; they actually sleep most of the day.

Seren normally threw a cloth over him. If he couldn't see what she was doing, he couldn't shout about it. Birdy only really spoke when she opened the front door or if there was a loud noise.

Seren thought about getting rid of him when her husband died, but she was sure he wouldn't survive in the wild. She often left the door open in the hope he would fly away on his own. If he had, she wouldn't blame herself if anything bad happened to him. But he would never leave; he just sat on his perch, shouting.

'IT LEFT THE DOOR OPEN FOR ME. IT'S TRYING TO GET ME KILLED.' Aderyn are clever birds.

While Birdy was shouting, Seren picked up her dishes from the kitchen table and walked to the window to snatch another glimpse of Fred. Yep, he was still there, looking angry.

'IT'S LOOKING OUT OF THE WINDOW.'

'Oh, shut up, Birdy,' she said, turning back to her dirty dishes. As she stood at the sink and started to wash them, Birdy shrieked, 'IT'S WASHING THE DISHES.'

Seren's kitchen was dark. She had tried to brighten it up when her husband died but failed miserably. Her idea was to create an extra window to let in more light, but she didn't realise that involved more than cutting a hole and knocking wood panels out from the side of the cottage. She only realised her mistake when the roof and most of the side of the cottage fell to the ground. So, the kitchen was still dark with a table and chairs, a kitchen sink, and counters. That's all she needed; it wasn't as if she entertained any visitors.

There were two doors to the left of the kitchen. One led to Seren's late mother-in-law's room and the second to the room she had shared with her late husband. Her room only contained a bed; that was all she needed. Seren knew it wasn't much, but she had never been happier.

The kitchen door led to the garden. The farm itself had two fields and a small back garden, with a handful of sheep in one field and Fred in the other. Chickens pecked in the back garden. This was not a livestock farm, well, not since her husband died. The sheep were more like pets. She had named them all, and the unwritten rule was, if she named them, they couldn't be eaten!

Birdy had fallen asleep; he was never awake for long. She put her things away and decided to feed the chickens. At the back of her garden, there was a forest, so thick with trees that no sunlight squeezed through. It was pitch black.

She opened the back door and left it open; this woke up Birdy. She heard him take a deep breath. 'IT'S TRYING TO KILL ME.' She rolled her eyes as she walked down the steps that lead to the garden.

Seren grabbed the bucket of feed and walked towards the chicken pen.

'Betty, Sarah, Roxy.'

All the chickens ran to her and she let out a small giggle. 'There you go, girls. You must be hungry.'

When she had finished feeding them, she turned back to the cottage, but a movement in the forest caught her eye.

'What was that?' she said out loud. The chickens looked at her as if they understood.

Betty looked like she knew the answer and dashed into the chicken coop.

Seren saw the trees move and heard an almighty screech. She dropped the bucket holding the chicken feed and ran into the cottage. She slammed the back door closed and fumbled at the key. Her breathing was heavy and her heart hammered.

What was that? She scanned the kitchen for something she could use as a weapon.

It was too loud to be one of her neighbours. Besides, they wouldn't come through the forest to get to her house, especially when they had been prewarned about the traps she'd put there. After her husband died, Seren felt vulnerable staying at the cottage alone, so she set up traps at the tree line.

She saw a knife on the kitchen table and ran to grab hold of it, then ducked under the kitchen window.

Holding the knife in both hands close to her chest, Seren raised her head slightly to peer out the window.

Nothing.

She scanned the tree line for any movement, but the trees were still. She pushed her head up against the glass to look left and right.

Still nothing. Fred was staring at the forest with his constipated look.

She sat back down, still clutching the knife in both hands.

It hadn't sounded like a human or an animal. What was it? A pounding on her front door was followed by a bellow, 'Open in the name of the king!'

Seren scuttled to hide under the kitchen table.

'IT'S HIDING UNDER THE KITCHEN TABLE. IT HAS A KNIFE,' screamed the aderyn.

After a few minutes, Seren emerged from under the table. Heart racing, she ran around the kitchen, looking for something. A hiding place or a secret door, maybe.

'IT'S DOING SOMETHING …' shouted the aderyn. he had been watching her run around the kitchen and was no doubt utterly confused.

'IT'S … UMM … FLAPPING ITS ARMS,' it screeched.

The knocking at the door stopped. Seren heard someone clear their throat. She stopped flapping her arms after realising it wasn't helping her situation.

'I'm a messenger,' the voice behind the door announced. 'I have been sent by the king to pass on a message to you, Seren Evans.'

Seren froze in the kitchen, utterly bemused. A message from the king and he knew her name!

She had no choice but to open the door. She took a deep breath and walked forward. 'IT'S WALKING TOWARDS THE DOOR ... IT'S STOPPED ... IT'S LOOKING AT ME ... IT'S PICKIN ... AAARGH,' and then he stopped.

Seren slowly opened the door and gasped. 'You're so cute!' she purred. 'You're a teeny, tiny, little fluffy wuffy messenger!'

The creature on her doorstep had long legs and a teeny tiny, little fluffy wuffy body. It was covered with fur, or possibly fluff. Whatever it was, Seren wanted to stroke it and hug it.

She took a step forward to pet him but stopped herself.

It was clear from the messenger's reaction that this was not the first time someone had called him 'cute'. He seemed neither offended nor pleased, but probably not sure how to take the *teeny tiny, little fluffy wuffy* remark.

He looked over Seren's shoulder at the kitchen and his eyes widened. Seren followed his gaze to the moving cloth on the perch.

'It's okay,' she said. She walked to the perch and pulled the cloth off the aderyn's head.

'IT THREW A TOWEL ON MY HEAD.'

'He gets a bit loud sometimes,' she said. 'And he's a liar,' she added quickly, remembering the knife in her hand. She flashed the messenger a smile. 'You have a message for me?'

The messenger cleared his throat. 'The king has sent me to inform you that your brother, Mr Simon Williams, has been arrested.'

Seren stared at the messenger, her mouth wide.

'He is currently being held in the jail at the Palace of Hiraeth.'

Seren's legs wobbled and her head spun.

'End of message,' declared the messenger. He put his hand into his pocket and pulled out a card. 'If you have time, could you possibly fill out this questionnaire?'

Seren took it without removing her glassy stare from the messenger.

'It's just a quick review about my professionalism,' he informed her with a broad grin. 'It won't take up much of your time. There's a return address on the back,' he added, pointing at the card.

Seren stared at him blankly.

'Well, then, have a good day,' he said and turned to leave.

'Wait!' shouted Seren.

The messenger stopped and turned back. 'It's just a performance review, and my name will be put into a raffle. I might win a prize.' He beamed.

Seren furrowed her brow.

'The more questionnaires that are filled out, the more chances I have of winning,' he explained, peering at her. 'It won't cost you anything to send it back; the postage is covered,' he added hesitantly.

Seren slowly shook her head. 'I don't …'

'Oh, silly me!' the messenger said, slapping his forehead. 'My name is Jim. You'll need to write it at the top.' He pointed to the top of the card. 'Right there.' He looked up at her. 'J-I-M.'

She didn't look at the card; she just stared at him, then shook her head roughly, as if to shock her brain into doing its job. 'Please could you repeat that?' she said slowly.

'Yes, of course,' he said, 'J-I-M, and it goes right at the top.' He pointed at the card again. 'Right there.'

'Not that part,' she snapped, then instantly regretted her tone. She felt like she had kicked a puppy. 'I'm sorry,' she said. 'Could you repeat the message about my brother?'

'Ah, yes, the message,' he said. 'The king has sent me to inform you that your brother, Mr Simon Williams, has been arrested. He is currently being held in the jail at the Palace of Hiraeth.'

She didn't reply.

Jim shuffled his feet. 'Would you like me to repeat it?'

'Um, no.' Her brain tried desperately to return to work, but it still wasn't fully functioning. She gave her head another quick shake.

'Why was he arrested?' she asked.

43

Ah, the brain is trying.

'I don't know,' he said.

'Why was he in the south?' she asked.

The brain is getting there.

'I don't know,' he said.

'Where's his wife?' she asked.

I don't know,' he answered.

Okay, back to normal brain function.

Jim seemed impatient to leave, yet lingered on the doorstep, seemingly torn between delivering other messages and getting a good review.

'I'm sorry I don't have any information,' he said gently. He lifted his hand and put it on her shoulder, either out of compassion or in the hope of getting positive feedback.

Seren tried to resist the urge to stroke him. She gave in and stroked is hand.

He was so soft and fluffy – or furry; she still wasn't sure.

Jim moved his hand away and brushed it on his chest, looking bashful.

'Um, I'd better be off,' he said.

Seren snapped out of her thoughts. 'Wait,' she said. 'Do you have any information at all about my brother?

'No, I'm sorry,' he replied.

Jim walked down the path and clicked open the gate. He started to jog down the road, then he picked up speed and, with an almighty screech, vanished. Seren stared at the dust swirling over the road.

Early the following morning, Seren walked past the cart and into Fred's field, holding a harness. Fred looked up.

He's not going to like this.

'Hello, Fred,' she said, trying to sound calm and reassuring. 'I've got something for you.'

Seren approached Fred slowly, raising the harness higher in the hope it would magically jump onto his neck.

Fred wandered a few paces backwards, eyeing her warily.

'It's okay, boy. I'm not going to hurt you.' She lunged at him.

After a struggle and some strong language from Seren – quickly followed by, 'I'm sorry, Fred, I didn't mean that,' – Seren stepped back to admire her hard work.

There stood Fred with the harness around his neck and strapped to his back. He looked out of breath; for a second, Seren thought he looked … embarrassed? No, sheep don't get embarrassed.

Seren yanked the harness to get Fred closer to the cart. Fred dug his hooves deep into the soil and grass, leaving tracks as Seren dragged him.

'Come on, Fred,' she said, trying to sound encouraging.

By the time Seren had harnessed Fred to the cart, she was out of breath and sweating. She flopped onto the ground, trying to catch her breath. Eventually, she got up and gingerly climbed onto the cart.

'Okay, Fred,' she said. 'It's time to go.'

She pulled on the reins.

'Let's go.'

But Fred was not budging. He stood still, ignoring her very existence.

'Let's go!' she shouted.

Seren tried every way she could think of to get him to move, but he was not having any of it. He turned his head in the direction of the other sheep, who were facing him, and he pulled at the cart.

'Well done, Fred,' said Seren. No doubt her words of encouragement were the reason Fred had moved. Sheep don't feel embarrassed. Do they?

Fred tugged the cart down the road and turned right, out of sight of the field of staring sheep. The rumbling wheels came to a halt.

'Come on, Fred. Let's move!'

Seren had studied the map of Hiraeth the night before. She had worked out it should take her eight days to get to the palace. She studied the map for resting places and rivers so Fred could get plenty of water.

The first village she would rest in for the night was Stoneshire. She'd never been there before, so she was unsure of where the stables were. They passed an older woman pegging out her washing.

'Excuse me,' called Seren from her cart. 'Where are the stables, please?'

'The stables?' the woman repeated, looking confused.

'Yes, the stables,' said Seren, smiling. Her mother had always told her that if she needed information from people, it was always better to smile; it makes people more forthcoming … apparently.

'You mean the stables for horses?' the woman said and started laughing. She lifted her arm and pointed at Fred. 'That's not a horse.'

'I know he's not a horse!' snapped Seren, frowning. 'I mean, yes, I know he's not a horse.' She forced a weak smile.

'They won't take in sheep,' the woman said. 'Peter! Come and look at this. It's a sight you'll never see again.'

Fred bolted off so fast that Seren nearly bounced out of the cart.

'Fred!' she shouted. 'Slow down!'

Fred was not going to slow down. He wanted out of this place. He missed his field, and this woman was making a mockery of him.

Tying him up like a mule to cart her around? Who the hell did she think she was?

Fred was running full pelt down the road. People were jumping out of his way.

I'm not stopping, no way. And I'm definitely not staying in any barn!

At the edge of Stoneshire, Fred came to an abrupt stop; so abrupt that Seren slid off the back of the cart and landed on the ground with a thud.

'What on earth?' she said as she stood and brushed down her dress. 'What happened, Fred?' She walked to the front of the cart and patted him like a dog. 'There, there. Something scared you, didn't it?'

Fred turned away. She thought he looked irritated. Maybe the harness had tightened and it was pinching him.

She looked around. 'We can stay here tonight. There's a stream over there. Right, let's get you out of that harness.'

She gently removed it, turned to take her bags out of the cart and heard him run. She gave chase, jumped on him and wrestled him to the ground.

'Hey, where are you going?' she asked as she tried to put a rope around his neck. 'It's not safe here, Fred. We don't know this place, and you'll get lost.' She eventually got the rope around his neck and tied the other end around a tree.

'There, the rope is long enough for you to reach the water,' she said, pointing to the stream. Fred stood immobile, staring in the opposite direction.

'Well, when you're thirsty, you'll go down there,' she said, smiling at the back of his head.

Seren set up camp for the night and lit a small fire. She looked over to where Fred

49

was standing. He still had his back towards her and wasn't showing any interest in this new place. Seren had thought that once they left the farm, he might at least have been inquisitive about the new places they visited, but he did not seem to be enjoying them at all.

She sat on a log, reached over and grabbed her travel bag.

'I've got something for you, look.' She pulled out a small transparent bag full of sugar cubes. 'Want one?'

Fred kept his back to her. Seren sighed, got up and moved closer to him.

'There you go,' she said as she moved her hand closer to his mouth. His lips remained clamped shut, so she dropped it on the ground.

'Well, it's there if you fancy a treat later,' she said, and walked back to her log.

Seren spent the evening examining Fred's harness, wondering why he shot off like that. She was sure it must have pinched him somewhere. After examining it thoroughly, she gave up and got into her makeshift bed. She rolled over to look at Fred, who was still facing the other way. She stared at him for a while before she finally fell asleep.

Seren was snoring so loudly that, at first, Fred thought a demon had taken over her body. On closer inspection, he realised it was her making the noise.

As he walked to the stream for a drink, he heard rustling from the top of a tree. A squirrel ran down the trunk and grabbed hold of the sugar cube. It seemed pleased with itself.

A CRAZY ENCOUNTER

The following morning, Seren woke up earlier than she would normally at home. She sat up and looked for Fred, but she couldn't see him. She shot out of her makeshift bed and ran to the tree where she had tied him, only to find him standing behind it.

She sighed with relief. 'Morning, Fred.'

Seren scoured the ground for the sugar cube, but it wasn't there. He must have eaten it during the night.

'Let's eat, then we'll set off again.'

After breakfast, Seren packed up her things and loaded the cart. She grabbed Fred's harness and slowly approached him.

Fred darted behind the tree. Seren pulled at the rope attached to his neck. 'Come on, Fred. We need to go.'

Seren could hear a woman shouting up the road. She seems to be arguing with someone. Seren let go of Fred and went to the edge of the clearing. She peered around the bushes and saw an elderly woman on her own. *Was she arguing with herself?*

The woman stopped and turned, lifted her arm and pointed to the air. 'I've told you before,' she shouted. 'I'm not telling you again.'

Seren rushed back to Fred. 'Come on,' she whispered. She didn't want to bump into anyone and start all that small-talk nonsense, especially people who argued with the air.

She struggled with Fred and had just managed to get the harness over his head when she heard the woman shouting, 'What are you doing?'

Seren lost her grip on Fred, and he dashed back behind the tree.

'Um ...' she started, 'I'm just leaving.' She turned and followed Fred behind the tree. Fred walked back around to where the woman could see him.

'Are you trying to put a harness on that sheep?' the woman asked.

'Er, yes,' said Seren, walking back in front of the tree and trying to grab hold of Fred.

'Shut up,' the woman said to the fresh air, then turned back to Seren. 'Not you, him.' She pointed to an empty space next to her.

'Oh, right,' said Seren, looking confused. 'Well, it was lovely meeting you.' She pulled Fred back behind the tree and out of sight.

'I don't think he wants to have that harness on,' shouted the woman.

'He'll be fine once it's on,' Seren called back. 'It was lovely meeting you.'

'Yes, I know that, you fool,' snapped the woman. She cleared her throat and shouted, 'Sheep don't normally pull carts.'

Seren, who was struggling with the harness, shouted back, 'Not normally, but it's an emergency.' She raised the harness to put it over the sheep's head. 'There, Fred.'

Fred shot back out from behind the tree. Seren slowly emerged too, sheepishly holding the empty harness.

'He's a sheep, girl. Why are you talking to him like he's a baby?' asked the woman.

'It doesn't cost anything to be kind to animals,' Seren snapped. She cleared her throat. 'It was lovely meeting you. Have a lovely day.' She pointed up the road, hoping the woman would take the hint.

'Yes, I'm well aware that she wants us to leave,' said the woman. 'Do you need help, girl?' she asked.

Seren judged her to be at least sixty. 'No, thank you.'

She turned back to Fred. She managed to get the harness over his head, but he

wriggled free and ran back behind the tree.
She fell to her knees, panting.

'You're sweating, girl,'

'He likes to put up a fight.'

The woman walked over to Seren and
snatched the harness off her.

'The trick is to be stern with animals,
show them who's boss and all that. He'll
never respect you if you keep talking to him
like he's a baby.' She marched behind the
tree.

Seren jumped up to stop her from
'showing him who's boss' and ran behind the
tree. The woman was tightening the harness
around Fred's belly.

Seren's mouth dropped open. 'How did
you do that?'

The woman shrugged. 'Showed him
who's boss.'

Seren looked at Fred to see if he was
hurt, but he just looked shocked and unsure
how he got into the harness.

'I'm Mavis,' the woman said and held out
her hand. 'And that's Fwl.' She gestured to
the air.

Seren looked at the space where Mavis
was looking, then turned back. 'I'm Seren,'
she said and shook Mavis's hand. 'And that's

Fred.' She nodded her head towards her companion.

'I gathered that,' Mavis said, looking down at him. 'You named him Fred?'

'Yes.'

'Why?'

'I was in a rush, and it was the first thing that popped into my head.'

'You were in a rush to name a sheep?'

'It's a long story,' Seren said self-consciously. She turned and tried to pull Fred towards the cart. He dug in his feet.

'Here,' said Mavis, taking the reins off Seren.

'Move!' she said to Fred sternly. Too sternly for Seren's liking.

She was about to tell her not to speak to him like that, when Fred moved towards the cart.

'Right, well, thank you for your help.' Seren looked at the empty space next to Mavis. 'Both of you.'

'Where are you travelling to?' asked Mavis.

'I'm going south to the palace,' said Seren.

'That's perfect,' said Mavis. 'I've been walking all night; I could do with a rest.' She pulled herself into the back of the cart and moved some of Seren's belongings to make herself a comfy spot to lie down.

'What do you mean?' Mavis said looking over her shoulder. 'I'm not imposing myself, I've just helped her with the sheep.'

'His name is Fred,' Seren said quickly. She scanned the air around Mavis again to see if any one was there. She knew there wouldn't be, but the old woman was convincing. Seren shook her head.

She stood next to the cart, watching Mavis moving all her things and talking to herself. Well, she's good with Fred, she told herself. Not kind, but she can handle his stubborn nature.

Seren climbed onto the front of the cart. 'Okay, let's go.'

Fred didn't budge, no doubt unhappy that he was attached to the cart again and about the extra weight to pull.

'Come on, Fred,' said Seren in a kind tone.

From behind Seren came a stern voice. 'Move!' Instantly Fred started to pull the cart.

Fwl sat at the back of the cart while Mavis slept. He had tried all night to convince her that going south and meeting with the Dewin was a bad idea. She was so stubborn. He'd said he could make her last years comfortable in a nice house, with a little garden. Somewhere that she could retire and relax.

He felt sorry for her, really sorry. He should have taken more notice of her and visited her more often, but he had so many other wards that she'd simply slipped through the net. And now look at him, travelling in the back of a cart pulled by a sheep.

Mavis stirred a little in her sleep. Fwl remembered the day she was born; she was so small and delicate. Her mother had just given birth and was dying. She made him promise to take care of her baby.

Fwl lifted his hand to his head. *I've failed her and broken a promise*.

They travelled in silence for most of the day. Every now and again, Seren would look over her shoulder to glance at Mavis. She was spread out like a starfish, mouth wide open. What a strange woman.

As Seren and Fred came around a bend in the road, she saw ... something. She wasn't sure what it was at first, but, as she got closer, she saw it was some kind of road block. Carts were lying on their sides.

'Fred, slow down,' said Seren.

'Who goes there?' shouted a man wearing a pointy hat.

'We are travelling south,' Seren called back.

'You can't pass through here,' said the man with the pointy hat.

'Why not?

'There are witches about. We've been told to block the roads and stop everyone from coming or going.'

Seren furrowed her brow. 'Why are you stopping people from leaving?'

Hurried whispering came from behind the road block.

'How will a wooden road block stop witches from passing? Surely they would just burn the carts and pass!' Seren hollered.

More rushed whispering came from behind the road block.

Fwl jumped off the cart and walked behind the road block. Five men in pointy hats were holding spears that bore the flag of Bridgestart.

Mavis shouted from the cart, 'What's going on?'

Fwl popped his head around the wooden carts and shouted back, 'I'm not sure, Mavis, but they have spears.'

'They've got spears?' she shouted.

'How does she know we've got spears?' one of the men whispered.

'They must have seen you, earlier, Roger,' said another man.

'You went for a pee!' said a third man. 'I told you not to go. I bet they've been watching us all day.'

'Don't be stupid,' said Roger. 'They haven't.'

'How do you know?' asked one of the men.

'Because we've just seen them come down the road.'

'They could have been hiding,' said the first man.

'We have a clear view of the road. Where the hell do you think they could have been hiding?' said Roger.

One of the men looked around the wooden road block.

'In the trees?' he asked.

'We need to ask where they've come from,' said Roger.

'What are they doing, Fwl?' Mavis called.

'Did she just call us a fool?'

'They want to know where you've come from,' shouted Fwl.

'Why do they want to know where we're from?'

'Oh my god! How does she know that's what we were going to ask?'

'Maybe she guessed?'

'They think you've been watching them all day,' shouted Fwl.

'Why would we want to watch them all day?'

'They think you've been hiding in the trees,' shouted Fwl.

'Hiding in the trees?'

'How can she hear us?'

One of the men gasped, 'She's a witch!'

'They think you're a witch,' Fwl called.

'A witch?'

From the cart, Mavis and Seren could hear the metal spears hitting the road and one man shouting, 'Run, boys, run!'

'Where are they off to in such a hurry?' asked Mavis.

Seren sat quietly in the front of the cart and didn't reply. Her uninvited companion was slightly creepy. Mavis knew what those men were saying but Seren couldn't hear anything.

'Who were you talking to?' she asked Mavis.

'Him.' Mavis pointed in front of the cart. 'Gone, have they? Let's get closer,' she said to the air.

Seren looked around, scratching her head. Maybe Mavis just had excellent hearing.

'Move!' shouted Mavis, and Fred instantly obeyed.

Seren and Mavis climbed out of the cart to examine the road block.

'We can just push them to the side of the road,' Seren said.

'That's easy for you to say, girl. I'm sixty-two!'

'Let's try.'

Seren and Mavis eventually succeeded in pushing the overturned carts to one side. Seren was impressed. Although Mavis was an older woman, she had the strength of two men. She didn't even break into a sweat. Seren walked back to her cart and lifted her bag. She untied it and pulled out her map. She sat on the side of the road to examine it. She knew the way, but she needed to catch her breath; that old woman put her to shame.

'There should be a stream further down the road,' Seren said. 'We need to stop for Fred to rest and have some water. He's been walking all day.'

'Okay,' said Mavis.

They found a clearing in the forest next to the stream. Seren unhooked Fred from the cart. She put the rope around his neck before she removed his harness. She had learned from her mistakes. Once his harness was off, she walked him to the stream and tied him to the tree nearest the water.

She looked back at Mavis who had found a comfy spot to sit, leaning against a tree.

Who does she talk to? How did she know they had spears?

Seren couldn't see or hear those men behind the road block, so how could Mavis?

Was she the witch? Don't be silly, a witch would have a black hat.

Seren turned to Fred. 'Sugar cube?' she said and bent down to stroke him.

Fred immediately stepped away. Seren walked back to the cart, grabbed her bag and pulled out the sugar cubes.

She looked at Mavis resting against the tree. 'How did you know they had spears?' she asked.

Mavis smiled, her eyes closed. 'Fwl told me.'

'I'll be careful from now on, Mavis,' Fwl said.

It was foolish of him to tell her what was happening. Those men and Seren knew that Mavis couldn't see through the road block. He'd never had to be her eyes and ears before. Seren was looking around Mavis to see who she was talking to.

Would Seren believe Mavis?

No one had believed her before, but Seren didn't see or hear the men behind that road block.

A big mistake.

'Mavis,' he said. 'Please, we should stop this now and go home. This will end badly for you. Can't you see that?'

'I don't care, Fwl. The only thing I care about is the truth,' she said, still leaning against the tree with her eyes closed.

'What truth?' asked Seren.

Mavis opened her eyes and looked at her. 'You're not in control of your own life. You know that, right?'

'What do you mean?'

'Mavis, please stop,' begged Fwl. 'No one will believe you; no one will *ever* believe you.'

'We are assigned so-called gods at birth and these gods control us.'

'We don't control you, Mavis. I've told you that. 'Gods?' Seren asked. 'I thought there was just the one for everyone.'

'Nope, not one for all of us. But lots of them running around, moving people here or there like chess pieces.'

Seren started to laugh.

'Believe it, girl. Gods. The most powerful gods get the most powerful families, like the royal family or rich people. It's a game to them.'

'How is it a game?'

Mavis grabbed hold of the tree with both hands and pulled herself up. 'What do you think happens when the gods get bored or disagree with each other?'

'I don't know,' said Seren, staring blankly at Mavis.

'That's how we get wars. Each god wants their people to be the best and have the best of everything. Land, power, gold, all of it.' She waved her arms above her head. 'And who do you think pays the price for these wars?' She leaned close to Fwl. 'We do.' She walked down to the stream, calling back, 'So, no, I will not stop, Fwl.'

'Mavis, that's not how it works!' he shouted after her.

Seren stood still, holding Fred's sugar cubes, her eyes following Mavis. For a second, Fwl thought that Mavis might have convinced her, but Seren shook her head and followed her to the stream.

'Are you saying I've got a god?'

'Wait a minute!' Fwl dashed after them. 'Mavis, don't, please. You'll just confuse her,' he pleaded.

'Yes,' said Mavis, ignoring Fwl. 'You've got a god.'

'And he controls me?'

Mavis stopped in her tracks, and turned to look at Seren. She'd never been asked any follow-up questions before. 'Yes, he or she controls you.'

Fwl caught up with the two women. He stood between them and turned to face Mavis. 'Stop this at once,' he demanded.

He wasn't sure if Seren was convinced and he started to panic. 'Mavis, please don't answer any more of her questions.'

Mavis waved her arms in front of her; they went straight through him. She knew he didn't like it when she did that. 'Out of the way, you fool.'

Fwl stepped out of her reach.

'And is Fwl your god?' Seren asked.

'Yes,' snapped Fwl, looking at Mavis.

'No,' retorted Mavis, looking back at him. 'He thinks he is, but he's not.'

'Is he … *my* god?' asked Seren.

Mavis looked at Fwl.

Fwl looked at Seren. 'She looks so sad,' he said. 'Why does she look so sad?'

'Well?' Mavis demanded. '*Are* you her god?'

Fwl turned back to Seren. 'No, she's not mine.'

'You're in luck, girl. He's not your god,' Mavis said.

A flash of sadness came over Seren's face.

Fwl cleared his throat. 'Please tell her the rest, Mavis. Don't leave her like that.'

Mavis turned to Fwl and said loudly, 'In my experience, they're not worth getting upset over. Angry, yes, but never upset.' She gave Seren a little smile.

'Mavis! You and I both know there is more to it than *control*,' Fwl said.

'Maybe you should nip off to find her god, and see if they're free for a chat about it.' She started laughing.

'It's getting late. We should set up camp for the night,' Seren said while Mavis was still chuckling.

'That's a good idea; I'm parched,' said Mavis. 'All this talking has given me a dry mouth. I'll get us some water.' She took Seren's water bottle and walked to the stream.

Fwl watched Seren as her gaze followed Mavis. *The poor girl*. He wondered why she looked so sad. He decided that, once he had got Mavis to change her mind about the Dewin, he would find Seren's god and see if they could cheer her up.

Seren lit a fire and started rummaging through her bag, 'Do you want a biscuit?' she asked Mavis, who was laying in her makeshift bed near the fire.

'No thanks, girl. I'm full.'

'Start a conversation with her, Mavis. Find out more about her,' Fwl said.

'Why?'

'Why what?' asked Seren.

'I was talking to him.'

'To get to know her. She seems lovely, and it wouldn't do you any harm to make friends,' he said, folding his arms and turning away.

'Why are you going south?' Mavis asked Seren.

'My brother is in the palace jail.'

'Oh, I wasn't expecting that,' said Fwl. 'It's fine, Mavis. Go to sleep; you've had a long day.'

'Why is he in there?'

'I think you can stop now, Mavis, and go to sleep. You look tired,' Fwl said.

'I don't know,' Seren replied. 'I was told yesterday that he had been arrested.'

'Are you close to him?'

'Not really. I haven't seen him in a long time.'

'Why are you travelling all that way if you're not close to him?'

'Mavis, don't be so insensitive,' Fwl said and shot her a look.

'I'm not being insensitive.' She looked at Seren. 'Am I?'

'No, it's fine. He's family; that's why I'm going.'

'And are your mam and dad going?'

'They're dead.'

'Stop now, Mavis. You don't do well with sensitive matters.'

Mavis ignored Fwl's request. 'Do you have other family?'

'No, it's just me and my brother. No, sorry,' she said quickly. 'He has a son. I keep forgetting about him.' She giggled quietly. 'I've never met him, so he always slips my mind.'

'Why have you never met him?'

'It's getting late. I think it's time to go to sleep,' Seren said kindly.

Mavis had lots of follow-up questions, but she was too tired to object. 'Goodnight, girl.'

'Goodnight, Mavis.' Seren rolled over to face Fred, then added, 'Goodnight Fwl. If you're really there.'

Fwl smiled. 'She's got a kind heart.'

A few moments later, Seren began to snore. Mavis sat up. 'My god, listen to her! It's the most deafening noise I've heard in all my sixty-two years!'

Fwl smiled. 'She is rather loud. Is that normal when people go to sleep? I'm not an expert or anything, but I'm sure that's not normal.'

Mavis lay back down and closed her eyes.

'Do you remember when you were younger, and Mrs Thomas crocheted you that blanket?'

'No.'

'It had been crocheted so perfectly and with so much care. You loved that blanket. You'd carry it everywhere and cuddle it every night in bed. It was red with green squares, remember?'

'Yes, now leave me to sleep!'

'Whatever happened to it, Mavis?'

'I burned it,' she said. 'I'm trying to sleep, Fwl.'

'Why did you burn it?'

Mavis sat up and looked at him. 'I'm not going to be keeping anything from people who you control. You whispered in her ear to take me in and crochet that blanket. Trying

71

to make yourself feel better for my miserable life.'

'No, no,' he said, waving his arms. 'Mrs Thomas took you in because she was kind. I didn't ask her to. She crocheted that blanket because she loved you, and she wanted to give you some comfort.'

Mavis lay back down. 'Stop lying, Fwl. Everyone I ever met was because of you whispering in their ear. Leave me alone. I'm trying to sleep.'

Fwl watched as Mavis got comfortable and slowly drifted off to sleep. He hadn't asked Mrs Thomas to take her in. She had done it because she was kind. He wished Mavis could see the good in people.

He sat all night and watched her sleep. It would have been a lovely night, if only Seren had stopped making that horrific noise.

ANOTHER MESSAGE

'Good morning, Mavis,' Fwl said with a wide smile.

'Shhh. It's too early for all that *chirpiness*.'

'Good morning, Mavis,' Seren shouted from the river. 'I'm just getting some water for breakfast.'

'She looks like she had a nice sleep; she didn't stop snoring all night,' Mavis said as she stood and began to gather her things.

'I know. I was here too,' he said flatly.

'You don't need sleep, so don't start complaining.'

'I still had to listen—, shh, she's coming back.'

'What's that horrible screeching noise?' Mavis said, covering her ears. It was getting louder and louder. 'What is it?'

Seren gasped. 'I know what it is. 'Jim!'

Her messenger appeared in front of them.

Seren instinctively lifted her arms to stroke him.

'Stop that,' said Jim, sounding annoyed. 'I have a message for Seren Evans.'

'How did you find me?'

'I have a message for Seren Evans,' he repeated.

'Yes, Jim, you already said that. But how did you find me here?' she asked again.

Jim cleared his throat. 'The king has set a date for the trial of Simon Williams. End of message,'

Seren glanced at Mavis, who was frowning.

'There must be more than that,' Mavis said. 'You didn't even give the girl a date.'

Fwl leaned into Mavis. 'Messengers are remarkable creatures; they'll find you anywhere. They just need a name and general area, and they'll find you.'

Mavis looked impressed. 'I've heard of them, but I've never seen one before. He's got fur, and look how long his legs are.' She chuckled.

'Who is she talking to?' asked Jim.

Seren whispered, 'She does that. She has, um, an imaginary friend. One that she doesn't seem to like much.'

Fwl gasped. 'Did you hear that, Mavis? She thinks you don't like me very much.'

'I don't.'

'What?' he said. 'Why not?'

'I'm not having this conversation with you again.'

'Anyway, I must be off,' said Jim.

'Wait! Do you have any more information about my brother?' asked Seren.

'No,' said Jim sharply.

'Are you okay, Jim?'

'Yes, thank you.'

'Are you upset with me?' Seren asked.

'Maybe it's because you haven't stopped smoothing him, girl.' Mavis laughed. 'I'd be upset too.'

'That's not the reason, but I would prefer it if you stopped,' Jim said. 'I'm upset because you didn't send back the questionnaire.'

'I'm sorry, Jim, I completely forgot,' she said. 'I was so worried about my brother, it must have slipped my mind.' She reached out to stroke his arm, but retracted her hand. 'I promise I'll send it as soon as I'm home again.'

Jim's face relaxed and, with a cheery goodbye, he gathered speed and disappeared with a screech.

Seren chewed her lip. 'I hope I get there in time. What if I miss the trial?'

'I don't think it will make much difference if you're there or not,' Mavis said.

'Don't be so unkind,' Fwl said. 'She's upset.'

'I'm not being unkind. I'm just saying he'll be tried and sentenced the same *with* or *without* her there.'

Seren looked at the empty space next to Mavis. Fwl thought she looked as if she was starting to become convinced.

'It's called 'moral support', Mavis. He's my family. Come on, let's pack up and get back on the road,' Seren said, still looking upset about Mavis's words.

Fwl watched Seren pick up her bag and swing it over the side of the cart. 'Mavis, maybe you should let her go alone. She might get there faster if we weren't with her.'

'What the hell does that mean?'
'What does what mean?' asked Seren.

'Do you mean I'm extra weight?' Mavis said, daring Fwl to answer.

He held up his hands. 'I never said that.'
'Then what did you mean?'

'I don't have time for this, Mavis,' Seren said. 'Just get in the cart. You can argue with him on the way.'

Mavis walked straight through Fwl. He hated it when she did that.

'You know that's not what I meant, Mavis.'

She climbed up onto the cart without replying to Fwl and shouted, 'Move, Fred.'

Just as Fred was about to take a step forward, Fwl jumped in front of him. 'I didn't—'

Fred jumped back and kicked the cart. Mavis and Seren were thrown back and landed on the ground behind it.

'My god, what happened?' Mavis asked, slowly getting up and rubbing the dirt off her dress.

'I stood in front of him and he jumped,' Fwl said, pointing at Fred.

'Can he see you?' Mavis asked, walking over to Fred.

'He hasn't reacted to me before.' He waved his arms in front of Fred. 'I don't think so.'

'Seren,' Mavis called. 'I think the sheep can see this fool. Seren?'

Mavis rushed behind the cart. Seren was lying on the ground.

'Come on now, girl.' Mavis lifted Seren's head and started tapping her face. 'Wake up. You don't have time to sleep.'

'I don't think she's sleeping, Mavis. She's unconscious.' Fwl knelt next to Seren. 'Will she be okay?'

'She'll be fine. Won't you, girl?' Mavis continued to tap Seren's face. 'You did this to her.'

'I didn't mean to. I didn't think Fred could see me.'

'What did you think was going to happen? Why jump in front of him like that?' Mavis snapped.

'For dramatics!' he said. 'I thought he would go through me, like everything else. How was I to know he could see me?'

'You did this on purpose. You've been trying to slow us down. Look at what you've done to her!'

Seren slowly opened her eyes.

What happened? Who's that man? How hard did I hit my head?

She tried to get up.

Mavis gently pushed her back down. 'Stay down, girl. You've had a bump to the head.'

Seren's eyes darted to Mavis, 'No, you don't understand.'

'Just rest for a minute.'

'There's someone behind you,' Seren said as she tried to get up again.

Mavis and Fwl stood and turned to look at the forest.

'There's no one there, girl,' said Mavis, turning back to Seren, looking confused.

'He's right there.' Seren lifted her arm and pointed at Fwl.

Fwl snapped around to look behind him. 'There's no one,' he said.

Mavis slapped one hand to her mouth and pointed at Fwl with the other. 'She can see you!'

Fwl stood, staring at Seren. She slowly got to her feet, keeping her eyes firmly fixed on him. 'Wait a minute,' he said. 'Let me think.'

'Is that him?' asked Seren. 'Is that Fwl?'

'Haha, yes, that's him, girl.' Mavis turned to Fwl. 'How you gonna talk your way out of this one, Fwl?' She chuckled.

'How can I see you?' Seren asked.

'Um, actually, I'd just walked out of the forest, just over there,' he said, pointing behind him, 'when I saw the two of you in

79

distress. So, I thought I would come and offer my assistance.' He smiled.

Seren pointed at the forest. 'You came out of there?'

'Ha! She's not going to fall for that,' Mavis said, laughing. 'Seren, meet Fwl.'

'This whole time you were real?' Seren said, looking at Fwl as if he were some sort of alien. 'Mavis, I honestly thought you'd lost your mind. I don't know how to process this.' She sank back to the ground and held her head. 'Everything you said was true? Gods controlling our lives?'

'Yep, they control us all.'

'No, no, no, that's not what we do,' Fwl said, waving his arms. 'Mavis only told you what she believes. She didn't tell you the rest … even when I begged her.' He shot Mavis a look.

'You've only got her version, Seren,' he said. 'Please let me explain.'

'Okay, then explain!' she snapped. 'Am I being controlled by you?'

Fwl leaned in front of Seren. 'No, of course not. We simply guide you to make good choices and only when you *ask* us for guidance.' He looked pointedly at Mavis. 'We don't get involved with your lives unless you *ask* us for help. And even when you ask, we would only whisper in your ear, to guide you.'

'Who is my god?' she asked.

'I'm sorry, I don't know,' he said. 'I haven't seen anyone with you the whole time we've been travelling. I thought I might have by now, but no one has been.'

'Should I be worried about that?'

'No,' he said, smiling at her. 'I don't think you've asked for guidance for a long time. You're doing great without any.'

'I'd be more worried if they started showing up to control you, if I were you,' said Mavis, sat on the log behind them and pulling off her shoes to clear them of little stones.

'We don't control you,' Fwl said, looking over his shoulder at Mavis.

'Why do you think they control us, Mavis?' asked Seren. 'I need to know which of you to believe.'

Fwl was a little hurt by her question. He must tread carefully with Seren. After the life that Mavis had led, he didn't want Seren to share the same fate.

'Mavis,' said Seren. 'Why do you think they control us?'

Mavis stopped shaking her shoes. 'It's the dreams I have.'

Fwl jumped up. 'What dreams? You've never told me about any dreams.'

'They're all in different colours, laughing and joking about what they've been saying to people,' she said.

Fwl gasped. 'How do you know about the colours? You've only met me and all your life I've been in yellow … well, except for the few moments after you were born when I was in blue, but you were too young to remember that.' He slapped his hands over his mouth.

'What did you say?' Mavis asked slowly. 'When I was born? You were there? When my mother died?'

'Ah, well, yes,' he said nervously.

'You've never told me this,' she said. 'Tell me the whole story … now!'

'Mavis, please, let's not get into this right now. Seren is having a crisis.' He turned and gestured towards their companion.

'What are you hiding from me, Fwl?'

'You hid your dreams from *me*.'

'Well, it looks like we both have our little secrets,' snapped Mavis.

'What if you're forgotten about? You know, accidentally,' Seren asked, rubbing her sore head. 'What if your god doesn't remember you exist?'

At that moment, the forest started to creak, and the wind rushed through the branches and leaves, pushing them almost to snapping point.

'What's happening?' Seren shouted.

The noises from the forest and the wind grew louder and louder. Mavis was pushed back by the wind.

'What is that?' she shouted, clamping her hand on her head to save her hat while her other hand grabbed onto the closest tree. She leaned into the wind, trying to keep her balance.

A loud pop reached their ears and the wind stopped.

Owain stood before them.

'Owain!' said Fwl, jumping back. 'What a pleasant surprise.' He grinned and slapped his hands together. 'Umm, what are you doing here?' He looked around at his companions. Of course, they couldn't see Owain. He realised he probably looked as crazy as Mavis had for all those years.

Seren and Mavis looked at each other and then at Fwl.

'Who are you talking to?' asked Mavis.

83

'Um … no one,' he said, looking sheepish.

'What's happening?' asked Seren. 'Who is Owain?

Mavis gasped. 'You're talking to another messenger from the devil!' She raised her arm, took two steps forward and pointed to an empty space next to Fwl. 'Now, you listen here, boyo,' she growled at the air. 'You'll not be controlling me! Do you hear me?'

'Mavis,' squealed Fwl. 'Stop, please.'

Seren looked around for somewhere to sit while she gathered her thoughts. That bump to the head had made her confused.

I'm just going to sit for a while.

She sank to the ground, leant against a tree and put her head in her hands. 'Could you please stop shouting for a minute?' she called.

She slowly reached out her arms, leant forward and crouched onto the ground. Lying flat on her back, she held her hands to her face.

'I just need to sleep for a few hours,' she said, 'then I'll be fine.'

'See what you've done?' snapped Mavis, pointing in Fwl's face. 'Look at the state of her!' She flapped her arms towards Seren.

'Now, hang on,' said Fwl, raising his hands defensively. 'Seren bumped her head. I didn't do it to her.'

Owain stood as still a rock, closely watching the trio.

'Fwl, it's been days, and you are nowhere near completing your task,' said Owain, turning towards Mavis. 'Not only have you not completed your task, but you've compromised us yet again.' He slowly moved his gaze to Seren.

'Owain, that was not my fault. She bumped her head,' Fwl protested.

'She is not your ward, Fwl,' said Owain. 'Now, this situation gets more complicated because she belongs to another god. Another god of Melyn, I believe.' Fwl looked at Seren. Owain was being rather judgmental about her. Just because she was dressed like that, it didn't mean she was the ward of a lower-level god.

'Right,' said Fwl slowly. 'What can be done about that? A letter of apology? Or I could visit … who was it again?'

'I don't know, Fwl,' said Owain. 'I'll make some enquiries and get back to you.'

Owain faced Fwl. His face was always serious but *this* face scared Fwl.

'I'm not sure I can help you this time,' the god of Du said. 'If her god sees fit to make a formal complaint, you will be demoted.'

'Owain, please!' Fwl begged.

'On the matter of Mavis …' Owain said, and they both turned to her.

'Don't look at me like that, Fwl,' she shouted.

'Please stop this noise,' said Seren, who was still holding her head and lying on her back. 'My head's killing me.'

Mavis stood with her hands on her hips, looking from Fwl to Seren.

'Right,' she said and walked to her bag. She pulled out a bottle and gave it to Seren.

'Here,' she said, 'drink this. It will ease the pain.'

'What is it?'

'Does it matter?' snapped Mavis. 'Just drink it.'

Mavis helped Seren to a sitting position and leaned her against a tree.

Seren looked at the bottle for a moment then put it to her lips.

'Fix this, Fwl. Make Mavis change her mind about the Dewin,' Owain said. 'In the meantime, I'll make some enquiries about Seren's god.' He walked a few steps and – *pop* – he disappeared.

Fwl rubbed his head. *How did this happen? I can't be demoted; I just can't!*

He was snapped out of his thoughts by a loud gasp from Mavis.

'Not all of it!' she cried, snatching the bottle from Seren. 'Oh my god, you drank it all!'

'I thought that's what you meant when you said, "Drink this." 'You didn't say, "just a few sips." You said, "Here, drink this." '

Mavis stood, holding the empty bottle and staring at Seren. 'Right,' she said slowly. 'Time for you to get some sleep.' She gave Seren a strange smile that wasn't at all comforting.

Seren lay on the ground and Mavis put a pillow under her head. 'You'll feel better after you sleep for an hour or so,' she said, patting Seren's shoulder.

It didn't take long for Seren to fall asleep. It didn't take long for her to start snoring either.

'How the heck is that noise coming from someone so small?' Mavis asked, turning to Fwl. 'Well, what did your *friend* want?'

'What friend?' Fwl said, attempting to look nonchalant.

'I think that's enough secrets between us,' Mavis snapped.

'I just need to think for a second. How could this happen again to Seren?'

'I hope you don't turn her life upside down as you did mine.'

Fwl's eyes grew wide. 'I didn't turn your life upside down! I tried to help you every chance I got.'

'How? Please explain. I can't wait to hear this.'

'I found good people to take you in after your mother passed away.'

'Do you know how many people I've stayed with in my lifetime?' Mavis asked, tapping her foot.

'Well, no, I didn't count them.'

'Twenty-seven. I've lived with twenty-seven people.'

Seren rolled over in her sleep and let out an almighty snore. Mavis and Fwl glanced at her, looking concerned.

He turned back to Mavis. 'Why does it matter how many people you've stayed with?'

'They all died.'

'That's not my fault!'

'It's not your fault they died, but it was your fault that I was surrounded by it.'

'What?'

'You placed me with older women, and every time one of them died, you would pass me on to another one.'

Fwl wasn't sure where she was going with this. 'But they were all lovely.'

'I'm not saying they weren't nice. What I'm saying is … it doesn't matter. You'll never understand.' She stormed off towards Fred. 'We need to get the harness off him. It doesn't look like we'll be going anywhere for a while.'

She fussed with Fred's harness a little longer than she had before. Fwl wondered if she had loved the women she'd lived with. It would explain a lot, but he didn't think she could love them fully, not with the little time she spent with each one. Now that he thought about it, he wondered if he'd been inadvertently cruel.

He gingerly approached her. 'I'm sorry. I thought I was doing the right thing.'

'Well, you weren't.' She turned to face him. 'By the time I was eighteen, I decided not to get close to anyone again. It hurt too much to lose them.' She glanced at Seren.

'I thought older women would share their experiences and teach you how to live on your own, you know, for when the time came.'

'They certainly taught me that.' Mavis finished untying Fred and walked him back to camp. She tied him to the tree nearest Seren. 'Right, Fred,' she said. 'You can stay there until she wakes up.'

Fwl noticed Mavis's kindness towards Seren.

'I'm going to collect more firewood,' she said. 'I think we'll be here a little longer than we thought.'

'What about her brother? She wants to get there before his trial.'

'I know, but as I said earlier, the trial will go ahead with or without her. Please watch her, and if she wakes up, call me. Don't go talking to her and feeding her nonsense.'

'Nonsense?'

'Yes, nonsense.'

Fwl watched Seren sleep, wondering how this new knowledge would affect her. He wasn't her god, so she might be fine. Once he had convinced Mavis to go home, he may never see Seren again. He wouldn't need to visit her as he did his wards. He put his head in his hands. This was new territory. It had never happened before, and he was beginning to worry about her. He shook his head.

She'll be fine.

While We Were Sleeping

Seren woke early the next morning to find Fwl's face hovering over hers.

He beamed. 'Good morning.'

She began to scramble away from him.

'Sorry, Seren, I didn't mean to scare you,' he said, raising his palms.

Mavis tutted. 'Of course that would scare her, you fool. You had your face right up to hers before her eyes were even open.'

She waved at Fwl to get him to move. Seren watched in wide-eyed horror as both Mavis's arms swished through him. A few seconds passed before Seren remembered the bump to her head. She tried to stand up, but Mavis gently held her down.

'Wake up properly first, then get up *slowly.* You drank a lot of the juice last night, so you're bound to feel dizzy today.'

'How long have I been sleeping?' Seren asked.

'Most of yesterday and all last night.' Fwl leaned next to her. 'How are you feeling?' he asked softly.

'My head hurts.'

'You had a nasty bump,' Mavis said.

'And you drank the whole bottle of Mavis's juice'—he turned to Mavis—'Let's not forget that.'

Seren stared, bleary-eyed, at Mavis and Fwl facing each other. What were they saying? Were they arguing? Seren's thoughts seemed to be stuck together. She wasn't thinking straight. She tried to focus on their words.

'And I told you last night it wasn't my fault. She hit her head first, *then* she drank the juice,' Mavis said.

'So it's all my fault?' Fwl said, throwing up his arms.

'Yes!' Mavis snapped.

Seren had the feeling she'd missed a lot of drama last night. It sounded like they'd been at each other's throats.

'Can you please stop shouting?' she asked. 'My head still hurts.'

'Sorry, Seren,' Fwl said, giving Mavis a dirty look. 'We knew you'd want to leave as soon as you woke up, knowing we've lost time here. We've managed to get everything loaded up, and breakfast will soon be on the go.'

Seren looked behind Fwl to see Mavis holding sandwiches. ' "We"? Did you say "we"?

'I was here as well,' he said.

'But *you* didn't do anything. *I* did it all,' Mavis said, gritting her teeth.

'That's because I can't do anything, but I offered you moral support,' he said in a matter-of-fact way.

Mavis huffed and walked through him.

'Mavis!' he groaned.

She ignored him and leaned towards Seren. 'If we travel most of today without any long stops, we might get to St David's by tonight. Let's get you up slowly.'

She reached under Seren's arm, 'Aren't you going to help, Fwl?' she chuckled. 'Some moral support would be a great help right now.'

Seren decided to ignore their bickering. Her head couldn't cope with it. 'Okay, let's go,' she said before they could start up again.

'This is nice, Seren, don't you think?' asked Fwl, sitting next to her at the front of the cart and flicking the reins to urge Fred to start walking.

Mavis had told them she hadn't had enough sleep the night before because the ground was so lumpy, so she made the back of the cart her new bed. Of course, she had been kept awake by Seren's snoring, but they weren't going to tell her that.

'Yeah, it's nice.' Seren took her eyes off the road for a second to glance at him. 'I'm not sure what to say to you. I thought Mavis had lost her mind when I first met her.'

'Ah, yes, she does give off the crazy vibe, when she talks to me. I've told her so many times, but Mavis doesn't listen to anyone. I always tried to visit her when she was alone because of the shouting, cursing and throwing things. It makes her look even crazier,' he said, smiling.

'But she was right. There *are* gods,' Seren said.

'Yes,' Fwl said.

'How can we both see you? Are there others who can?' Seren asked.

He shook his head. 'Mavis is the first known case.' He leaned closer. 'Until now.'

'But how?'

'We tried to find out when it first happened but failed to find a logical reason.'

'You stopped looking for the answer?'

'Yes.'

'And now there are two of us?'

'Uh-huh.' He smiled.

Seren chuckled. 'Maybe you shouldn't have stopped looking for the answer. I banged my head, and when I woke up, I could see you. Maybe there's a part of my brain that was hurt, you know, and it's just a little bruised. I might not be able to see you again when that bruise heals.'

He stroked his chin. 'Possibly.'

'So, did Mavis bump her head when she was a baby?'

'No, she—'

'Will you two stop wittering on? Honestly, you're so loud, you could wake the dead!' Mavis said from the back of the cart.

'Sorry, Mavis.' Seren looked at Fwl and they both burst out laughing.

After they had calmed down and Mavis had drifted back to sleep, Seren whispered, 'Do you watch all the people you're in charge of?'

'In charge of? We're not in charge of anyone. I think Mavis gave you the wrong impression. We guide people. It's up to them really if they follow it through or not. We don't force them.'

There was a moment of silence, then Seren said, 'If I was struggling to make a decision, how would I ask for help?'

'You know, I failed miserably when I tried to explain all this to Mavis, and I don't want to make that mistake with you. I don't want you to share the same fate, so to speak. I promise if you give me time to think about what I need to say, then I'll give you all the answers to your questions,' he said quietly.

Seren glanced at him. 'You can take your time; I'm already overwhelmed.' She shot him a wide smile.

Fred's hooves clopped on the dusty road. Seren gazed at the countryside, deep in thought. 'You care for Mavis a lot.'

'She's my ward. I love her very much,' he said.

'She doesn't seem to feel the same way about you,' Seren said, laughing. 'When I woke earlier, I saw Mavis put her arms through you.'

Fwl frowned. 'I hate it when she does that.'

'Does it hurt?' Seren asked.

'No, it's just uncomfortable.' He leaned closer and whispered, 'It's also very rude.'

97

'If you can't touch things, how are you sitting on the cart?' she asked.

Fwl chuckled. 'I'm not actually sitting; this is a little trick I learnt for Mavis. I'm sort of hovering over it. I learnt to do it when Mavis was younger. She was always looking up at me. I thought she might snap her neck the way she was bending it back when she spoke to me. So, I started to, sort of, pretend to sit with her.'

'You're doing a great job. It looks like you're actually sitting.'

'Thank you.' He flashed a wide smile. 'It took me a long time to learn. I spend hours watching people just sit.'

'Look,' Seren said, staring ahead.

In the distance, there was an overturned cart. Its occupants were standing by the side of the road, waving.

'I think they need help,' Seren said.

'Who?' said Mavis, popping her head up in between Seren and Fwl.

Seren jumped. 'Jesus Christ, Mavis!'

'Language, Seren,' Fwl said.

'Sorry.'

'Who needs help?' Mavis asked again.

Fwl pointed ahead. 'Them. It looks like their cart has flipped on its side.'

'How the hell did that happen? Can't we go around them?' Mavis said.

'Why would you want to do that, Mavis?' Fwl asked.

'We don't know who they are. They could be robbers, for all we know.'

'They need help,' Fwl said.

'That's okay for you to say, isn't it? It will be us that's helping them, while you stand on the sidelines, giving *moral support*,' Mavis said, mockingly.

'What do you think, Seren?' Fwl asked, ignoring Mavis's remarks.

'There's no other route, so we've got to pass them. We'll ask if they need help.'

Fwl sat at the front of the cart, grinning.

Seren slowed Fred down as they approached the occupants of the cart, a young man and woman. Their simple farming clothes were threadbare and faded, just like Seren's.

'Do you need any help?' Seren asked.

'Yes! Why do you think we were waving like that?' snapped the man.

'That was goddamn rude,' Mavis said.

Fwl glared at her.

'He started it, didn't you hear him? What a cheek,' Mavis said in a shocked tone. She turned to her companions. 'I think we should leave.'

Just then, the young woman walked over to Fred and stroked his head. 'His name is Fred,' Seren said, clenching her teeth. 'And he doesn't like it when people do that.'

The young man circled the cart.

'What are you doing?' Mavis snapped at him.

'Just looking at this fine cart of yours, old lady.' He smirked at her.

Mavis let out a loud gasp. 'How dare you!' she said, scrambling to stand up.

'Come on, Fred,' Seren said quickly, before Mavis properly got into her stride.

Fred jumped into action and walked forward. Mavis stumbled. She was red in the face with anger. 'You only asked if they needed help; there was no need for rudeness.'

'Some people are a li …' Seren started to say. 'Um, a lit …'

Fwl looked at her. 'Are you okay?'

'I don't feel well.' She looked at Fwl, her eyes closed slowly, and she slumped forward in her seat.

'Seren!'

The cart jerked. Fwl looked over at Fred only to find he was lying on his side, out cold.

'Mavis, something's wrong!' He turned in his seat to find his ward lying face down.

Fwl looked around wildly for help, but no one else was around. The young man and woman raced down the road towards Fwl's companions.

'Please help my friends,' he said, knowing they couldn't hear him.

'That was fast,' said the man. 'Did you sprinkle too much powder?'

'It was an accident. The sheep made me nervous,' said the woman.

'What on earth is happening?' Fwl said to absolutely no one.

The man climbed up and pushed Seren into the back. She landed on Mavis with a thud. He walked to the front of the cart and poured liquid from a vial onto Fred's face.

'What are you doing to him?' Fwl demanded. 'Let him be!'

'Come on, little fella,' the man said. Fred stirred and slowly opened his eyes.

'It's okay, Fred,' Fwl said in what he hoped was a calming voice, even though he knew Fred couldn't hear him.

Wait a minute, he can see me. Well, he could when Seren bumped her head. If Fwl could startle Fred, he might make a run for it with his friends in the back. It would give Fwl time to wake them up.

He stood in front of Fred. 'Go!' He started gesticulating in the sheep's face. 'Go on!'

Fred didn't respond.

'Fred, look,' shouted Fwl as he took a run at him. Fred didn't even flinch as Fwl ran straight through him and stopped in the middle of the cart.

Fwl flopped his arms to his sides. 'But, you saw me once.'

'Is he awake?' asked the woman.

'Yeah, let's give him a minute, though,' the man replied.

Fwl returned to Fred. 'Listen, our friends are in trouble. They need your help. Go!' he shouted and swung his arms in the direction of the road.

Fred started moving forward.

'That's it! Well done, Fred!' Fwl straightened up and saw the two interlopers sitting in the cart, the man holding the reins.

'No!' Fwl said. He watched in despair as the cart took the kidnappers and his companions away.

What do I do now?

He took a deep breath and shouted, 'Owain, please, I need your help!'

No one came.

He couldn't go to Carwen, as Owain had said he couldn't go back and that he needed to spend every moment with Mavis. But she was out cold, so he could technically nip over to Carwen and see if Owain could help.

No, I'll stay with Mavis. That's my task.

Fwl blinked, and he was back on the cart with Mavis and Seren. He watched over them as they travelled through the countryside. Eventually they entered a forest and came to a large clearing.

'Woah, boy,' the man said.

Fwl looked around. Wooden caravans of all shapes and sizes filled the clearing.

He closed his eyes and appeared next to Fred. 'Are you okay?'

Fred completely ignored his very existence. That was a mystery to solve another time.

'What you got there, mush?' shouted a voice behind Fwl. He turned to see a tall muscular man with jet-black hair walking towards the kidnappers.

'I found some strays out on the road, Carl,' the male kidnapper said.

'Did they give you much trouble?' Carl asked.

The kidnapper smirked. 'Na, piece of cake.'

'I've never seen that before, mush. A sheep pulling a cart.' Carl looked at Fred with amusement.

'It's a first for me, too. He's as strong as an ox.' He bent to rub Fred's head.

'Hey, Sarah,' Carl shouted over his shoulder. 'Come and have a look at this lot.'

A woman emerged from the back of one of the caravans. She was wearing a shiny white blouse and a multi-coloured long skirt. She had her long brown hair pulled back into a ponytail. 'What?' she said.

'Come and have a look, mun,' Carl said, beckoning at her.

Sarah approached and saw Fred attached to the cart. Her mouth widened into a smile. 'Did you do that, mush?' she asked the kidnapper.

'No, he was already like that.'

They started to laugh so loudly that others emerged from their caravans and walked to the clearing.

The whole clearing rang with laughter. Fwl looked at Fred, who didn't appear happy at all. He tried to make a run for it.

'That's it, go on, Fred, run!' Fwl shouted.

It took four men to grab his harness and reins, and after a long struggle, they brought him to a stop.

'I'd best unhook him and tie him with the horses,' the kidnapper said.

Fred tried running again, and all the men scrambled to grab him. Once Fred was unhooked and his harness removed, he was tied to a tree next to several horses. He did not look happy.

Fwl stood next to the cart and looked at his companions.

Okay, Fwl, what are you going to do about this? Think, think.

He tapped his head.

The residents of the camp had moved away and settled around the campfire. He crept over to listen to their conversation.

'And then what happened, mush?' Carl asked.

'She said, "That was goddamn rude." If looks could kill, I'd be lying on the road right now!' The kidnapper started laughing.

Fwl walked around the camp to find anything that could help him. He knew there wasn't much *he* could do until they woke up, but he could investigate possible exits or something they could use to escape. He heard a noise behind one of the caravans. Someone was whispering. He walked around and saw a young boy leaning on the caravan. His eyes were closed tight. 'Please, what should I do?' he was whispering to himself.

This is it! This young man is asking for help; someone will be here soon.

Fwl felt helpless watching his pleas.

'Please, please, what should I do?' the young man whispered again.

There was a loud popping noise and there stood …

'Gwen!' shouted Fwl.

Gwen, a god of Melyn, stood before him, dressed in a smart yellow suit. Her thick curly brown hair framed her friendly face.

'Fwl?' What are you doing here?' she said, her eyes wide.

'Gwen, you have no idea how happy I am to see you,' he said. 'I desperately need your help.'

He spent a few minutes explaining what had happened to his companions.

'So, you can't leave her?' Gwen asked.

'Owain told me I had to stay with her,' he said.

'Please, what should I do?' said the young man.

'Maybe you should help him first,' Fwl said, looking at the young man.

'This is Garry,' Gwen said, smiling. 'He has some issues mingling with people. Social gatherings and all that.'

'Right. And what help is he asking for?' Fwl said, frowning.

'He has something called "social anxiety"; he gets in a right old state if he knows he's got to be social.'

'I've never heard of that.'

Gwen leaned close to Garry's ear. 'You'll be fine; go and be social. It. Will. Be. Fine.' She smiled at Fwl. He loved seeing someone else at work. Garry took a deep breath and said out loud, 'I'll be fine.'

Fwl clapped. 'That was excellent work.'

'Thank you,' she said with a curtsy. They watched Garry walk over and joined the residents of the camp.

'Right, let's see about your situation,' Gwen said.

Both closed their eyes tightly, then disappeared and reappeared next to Seren and Mavis.

Gwen looked at them. 'Gosh, they're out cold.'

'Yes, and Mavis is in her sixties, so I'm a little worried about how her body will cope with this,' Fwl said, his brow furrowed.

'Was it a sleeping potion?' Gwen asked. 'I believe so.'

'That's a dangerous potion to brew. I wonder who did it?' Gwen studied the group surrounding the campfire.

'I don't have time to find out. What should we do?' Fwl said.

'We could use Garry to help, or I could try and find Owain.'

'Garry first. I don't think Owain is happy with me right now.'

Fwl hadn't told Gwen that Seren could see him. It was one thing for his ward to see him but quite another for a different god's ward. 'You don't happen to know who young Seren's god is, do you?'

'I don't, I'm afraid,' Gwen replied.

Well, that's one god of Melyn off the list, Fwl mused.

Gwen walked over to Garry. Fwl watched as she whispered in his ear.

Garry immediately stood and walked to Fred, untied him and led him to Seren's cart. Fwl watched the residents of the camp anxiously.

Please no one look over here.

'My heart is racing, Gwen,' he whispered.

'Why are you whispering?' Gwen laughed. 'They can't hear us, remember?'

'It's just the suspense,' Fwl said, rubbing his hands.

'Oi, mush!' one of the men shouted. 'What the hell you doing?'

Everyone at the campfire stood to see what the man was hollering about.

'Mush!' he bellowed again.

Fwl saw that Garry had almost got Fred's harness attached, but Fred was putting up a fight.

'Come on, Fred,' Fwl said encouragingly. 'For Seren.'

Fred immediately stopped fighting and allowed Garry to fix the harness.

'Did you see that, Gwen?' Fwl shot a look at Gwen.

'How did you do that? Is Fred yours?' she asked.

'No, he's not,' Fwl said. He bent to Fred and smiled. 'Good boy.'

'Oi, mush!' The man grabbed hold of Garry and threw him to the ground. 'What are you doing?'

'I'm letting them go,' Garry said.

'Why?' the man asked, rage in his eyes.

'I don't know,' Garry said.

'Get back over there, and stay away from the sheep.' The man yanked Garry up by the arm and pushed him towards the campfire.

'Okay, so that plan didn't work,' Gwen said as they both watched Garry being marched back to the fire. 'What next?'

'I don't want to ask Owain for hel—'

Garry rushed through Fwl, scrambled onto the cart and grabbed Fred's reins. 'Go, boyo, go!' He pulled the reins so hard that Fred jumped into the air and hit the ground running.

Fwl's mouth fell open. 'Did you see the froth around Garry's mouth?'

'Yeah, what was that about?' asked Gwen.

'I don't know. He seemed feral for a second; out of control,' Fwl said.

Fwl and Gwen squeezed their eyes shut and appeared in Seren's cart. Gwen leaned into Garry's ear. 'Go a little further south.'

She sat next to Fwl who was looking at Mavis. He was concerned about her. She wasn't the healthiest person, and he didn't know what this poison would do to her.

'I'm sure she'll be fine, Fwl,' Gwen said. 'I'll ask Garry to stop soon; I don't want him too far from his family. I'll go back with him to make sure he's okay.'

'Thank you for your help today, Gwen. I would never have been able to help them without you.'

'It wasn't me; it was our brave hero, Garry.' She looked at her ward and smiled. Fwl knew how Gwen felt. He felt the same about Mav— well, any of his other wards.

'I think this is far enough, don't you?' Gwen asked after a while. 'It will be getting dark soon. I don't want him too far from home.'

'Of course. This is a good place to leave us,' Fwl said, looking at the patch of grass by the side of the road.

Gwen leaned over and whispered in Garry's ear to stop. Fwl watched Garry climb out, looking confused.

111

'Thank you again, Gwen.' Fwl paused for a second. 'Could you keep this, umm, little encounter between us?'

Gwen nodded. 'No problem. It was lovely seeing you again.'

She and Garry walked down the road and out of sight.

Fwl looked at his unconscious companions. Seren was leaning on Mavis. His ward didn't seem to be in any discomfort; it just looked like she was sleeping.

An almighty roar came from Seren.

'Ah!' Fwl nearly jumped out of his skin. He held his hand to his pounding heart and stood up straight. How could such a small girl make such a loud noise?

Fwl appeared next to Fred. 'Can you hear me, Fred?'

The sheep didn't show any sign of seeing or hearing Fwl. How strange.

Fwl put his face close to Fred's so they were eye to eye. 'Can you see me?'

Nothing.

'What was that about back there?'

Nothing.

Fwl watched over his companions all night. Seren's snoring was like a hammer hitting his brain. He couldn't untie poor Fred, so the sheep had no choice but to sleep in his harness, hooked up to the cart.

Once the early rays of sunshine peeked over the horizon, Seren started stirring. Fwl sat up and waited for her eyes to open.

'Thank goodness!' he exclaimed.

He was happy she'd finally woken up and seemed unharmed by the poison, but he was even happier she'd stopped snoring.

'What happened?' Seren asked. 'Why am I here?' She pushed herself up and off Mavis.

'I'll tell you in a minute, but firstly, Fred is fine, just a little annoyed he slept in his harness all night. And please take a look at Mavis!' He said this clearly so that Seren wouldn't fuss over Fred. Fwl needed her attention on his ward.

Seren threw a quick glance at Fred, then, much to Fwl's relief, she turned to Mavis and loudly called her name. She grabbed hold of the old woman and shook her. 'Mavis!' she shouted again.

Mavis started to stir and opened her eyes slowly. 'What the hell is happening?'

Fwl let out a sigh of relief. 'Honestly, I thought for a second she wasn't going to wake up.' He covered his face with his hands.

113

'Are you okay, Mavis?' Seren asked gently.

'What the hell happened?' Mavis demanded.

Fwl moved his hands from his face and started laughing uncontrollably.

'What's so funny?' she snapped.

'Ah, Mavis. I'm glad you're awake.'

He closed his eyes and disappeared then reappeared next to Fred. 'Before I answer any questions, I'd like to request that Fred be taken out of that contraption. He would also like to be fed and watered. Then he would like a nap.'

'How do you know that?' Mavis asked, brow furrowed.

'That's a question, Mavis. And I will not be giving any answers until my demands are met.' He folded his arms. 'Let's go.'

After tending to Fred, Seren and Mavis sat down as Fwl told them what had happened.

'So, do you think Fred heard you say my name and wanted to help me?' Without waiting for Fwl's reply, Seren shot up and ran to Fred to try and hug him. He wriggled free of her grasp.

Fwl and Mavis watched. 'Do you think she knows he hates her?' asked Mavis.

'I don't think she cares. She loves him. She will keep him safe, and that's all that matters,' said Fwl. 'And I don't think he hates her. If he heard me last night, he stopped fighting Garry because of her.'

Mavis pouted. 'He looks at her like he hates her.'

'That's a strong word. I think he just doesn't like her very much,' he said.

'That's the same thing,' Mavis retorted.

'It's not. If he hated her, he would try to bite her.' Fwl frowned. 'I think that's what animals do?' He turned to Mavis. 'I think he tolerates her. It is strange how she's so overprotective of him.'

Fwl and Mavis watched as Seren struggled to keep Fred in her grasp. She finally gave in and joined her companions.

'So, for half a day and a full night we were sleeping?' Seren said as she sat next to them.

'Well, technically, for half a day you were unconscious because of the potion. That potion didn't send you to sleep; it was something else. It changed to sleeping from late last until you opened your eyes this morning,' Fwl said.

'How do you know?' Seren asked.

'Just a guess.' He shot Mavis a look and mouthed '*Snoring.*' She started laughing.

'That's a lot of time to lose,' Seren said.

Fwl beamed. 'Yes, but everyone is safe and well.'

'We'll try and make up for lost time, girl,' said Mavis.

'Do you know where we are, Fwl?' Seren asked.

'I believe we might be to the south of St Davids. The kidnappers took you around the village, and Garry brought you here.' Seren got up and grabbed her bag. She fished out the map of Hiraeth.

'If we leave now, we could get to the next village, The Bryn, by nightfall. We could rest there for the night. And then, look'—she pointed to the map—'we'll be nearly halfway there.'

Fwl saw the concern on her face when she looked back at the map. 'I'm sure your brother is fine, Seren.'

When she looked at him, her eyes were brimming. 'If you happen to have a conversation with one of the other gods

116

again, would you ask them about Simon? You know, just ask if he's okay?'

'You could have asked your friend two days ago,' Mavis said, shaking her head.

He shot her a stern look. 'I didn't think of that, with all the chaos around Seren seeing me and all.' He turned to Seren. 'Of course. I'll ask Owain.'

'Right, time to go,' Seren said and packed her stuff away.

A GOD OF ... NOTHING?

Owain stood in his empty office looking out of the window. He felt uneasy. He wasn't keen on this plan.

'Are you sure this is wise?' he said out loud to his empty office.

'*Yes*,' came the reply.

'What if something goes wrong?' Owain asked.

'*It won't.*'

Owain sighed.

'*You are concerned?*' the voice asked.

'A little.'

'*You don't have faith in my plan?*'

'It's not the plan I have issues with.'

'*You must have faith in him.*'

'He might get hurt.'

'*He will not be unprotected, Owain.*'

'He will be vulnerable.'

'*No harm will come to him.*'

Owain shook his head, closed his eyes and disappeared from his office.

'We have to stop. Fred needs rest,' Seren said. 'We can't be far from The Bryn, so let's set up for the night.' She stopped the cart and looked around.

'Down there,' Mavis said, pointing.

Seren followed the line of her finger to an off-road path, wide enough for the cart. Seren shook the reins and Fred walked down the path.

'This will do,' Seren said as she pulled Fred to a stop. 'I'll unhook him and take him for a drink at the stream.'

As Seren walked away with Fred, the wind picked up and there was a loud *pop*.

Fwl jumped back as Owain appeared in front of him.

'Lovely to see you again, Owain,' Fwl said.

'I have made enquiries with regards to Seren's god.' They looked at Seren, standing with Fred at the stream. 'Unfortunately, I have been unable to locate them.'

'How strange,' said Fwl.

'Indeed.'

Owain looked at Fwl. 'You are not going to like what I'm about to say.'

Panic shot across Fwl's face. 'Am I being demoted?' He clutched his chest with both hands.

'Not at the moment; however, I won't lie, there is talk of it. We will cross that bridge when we get to it,' Owain said in a low voice.

Mavis watched Fwl have this one-way conversation, as Seren and Fred rejoined the group. Fwl turned to them. 'I'm not being demoted yet.' He tried to sound reassuring, but it was more for him than for them.

'That's good news,' Seren said. 'Did he find my god?'

Fwl gave a watery smile. 'Not yet, but I'm sure it won't be long.' He turned back to Owain. 'What won't I like? I'm sure I'll be fine with what you're about to tell me, if it's not demotion.'

'Your attempts with Mavis are not working.'

He glanced at his ward. 'Not yet, no,' he said slowly.

Mavis couldn't see or hear Owain, but Fwl's expression unnerved her.

'The gods of Popeth have decided you will spend the next few days as a human,' stated Owain.

Fwl's head snapped back to Owain. '*I beg your pardon?*' He held up his palms. 'I'm sorry, Owain, I don't know what came over me, but please, I can't live as a human!'

'You must plead with her, Fwl,' said Owain in a calm voice.

Both Owain and Fwl stared at Mavis as she shouted all kinds of obscenities at the air next to Fwl.

'You must connect to her human side. It's been decided.'

'Please, Owain,' begged Fwl. 'I don't know how to survive as a human.'

'It's done.'

Fwl grabbed hold of his throat and started to gurgle. 'Please, Owain, the pain.'

'What's happening to you?' snapped Mavis as she reached out to touch his shoulder. She gasped. 'My hand touched you!' she shouted.

'Fwl,' said Owain. 'You've been human for exactly thirty-two minutes. It was a painless transformation. Get on with the job at hand.' He turned and walked out of the forest.

Fwl dropped his hands to his side and lowered his head.

'How can I touch you?' asked Mavis, patting him harder and harder.

'Stop, Mavis, please. That hurts.' He pulled away from her.

'Hurts?' she repeated.

'Yes.' He stared at her for a moment, then burst into tears.

121

Mavis stood slowly, not taking her eyes off Fwl.

'Are you human now?' she asked.

Fwl howled.

'Why have they done this to you?' asked Seren.

'Is it a punishment or have they just given up on you and kicked you out of their club?' asked Mavis, giggling.

'Neither. They think I'll be able to convince you not to see the Dewin if I'm human,' Fwl said through sobs.

'Well, that doesn't make any sense,' said Mavis. 'Human or not, it won't change my mind.'

Mavis stared at Fwl, wondering how anyone thought it would make a difference. She was going to the Dewin. End of. She watched Fwl slowly rub the bark of a tree next to him, then he picked up speed. His face lit up.

'I can feel everything!' He put his hands flat in the dirt and rubbed. He grabbed a handful of flowers and pulled them out of the ground. He took a long sniff. 'These smell beautiful! Here, sniff them.' He got up and thrust the flowers under Mavis's nose.

'Get them out of my face,' she snapped, pushing his arm away.

He thrust them at Seren. 'Smell them!'

She took a sniff and smiled at him. 'They are beautiful.'

'Is this your first time being a human, or do the gods often do this sort of thing?' Seren asked.

Fwl stared at her. 'As far as I'm aware, I'm the first one,' he said.

He touched Seren's arm. 'Your skin is so soft. I imagined it would be.' He darted to Mavis and touched her arm. 'Oh, that feels … different,' he said, frowning.

'I've got a lot more years on me than she does,' Mavis said defensively. 'Now get off.' She pulled her arm away.

'What should I do first?' he said excitedly. This is an amazing opportunity! I'll be able to tell all the gods about my experiences. You know, what things feel like or smell like.' He lifted up the flowers in his hand again.

'What happens if you fail to convince Mavis?' Seren asked, wrinkling her forehead.

Fwl stopped in his tracks. 'I don't know. I'm hoping we'll never find out.'

Mavis rolled her eyes. 'Come on, let's get going.'

'What is that?' shrieked Fwl, clutching his hands to his chest.

'A little spider.' Seren seemed to be holding back her laughter.

'It's disgusting! Get it off me.' he screamed and shook his leg vigorously.

Seren calmly walked over to Fwl and wiped the spider off his leg.

He let out a long breath. 'Thank you.' For a second I thought I was going to die.' He reached out to pat her shoulder.

'It was just a spider, Fwl. It won't hurt you.'

'How will I survive this?' He put his hands on his head. 'As beautiful as Hiraeth is, it comes with its dangers.'

'We need to pack up our things,' Seren said. 'Let's get them on the cart.' She rubbed his back reassuringly and handed him a small bag.

He took it and dropped it immediately. 'What's in there?' he asked, looking at it and rubbing his arm.

'It's just the blankets,' she replied, bending to pick it up, 'It's not that heavy.' She handed it back to him.

He kept hold of it this time, but he lowered it to the ground and dragged it towards the cart.

Mavis watched him drag the bag, taking deep breaths with every pull.

'The way he's acting, you could swear it's full of rocks,' she said to Seren. 'Look, he's actually sweating,' she said, raising her voice.

'You should be kinder to him,' said Seren. 'He's going through a lot right now.'

'Kinder?' snapped Mavis. 'To *him*? 'Listen, girly, your world is about to get a lot harder because of him.'

'How?' asked Seren. 'He's not doing me any harm.'

'Not yet,' said Mavis. 'But he will. He might not mean it, he'll have good intentions and all that, but he's a fool ...' She leaned into Seren and whispered, 'You need to remember he doesn't care as much as he thinks he does.'

'What does that mean?' Fwl said, walking back to them. 'Of course I care!'

Mavis took a deep breath, her face turning cherry-red. 'Stop telling me you care!' she shrieked, pointing her finger in his face.

'But I do. I care very much about you,' Fwl said, outraged.

Mavis turned away for a moment. She needed to gather her thoughts. She turned to look at him.

'Do you remember when I was seven and you thought I wasn't eating enough green vegetables? You whispered in Mrs Joyce's ear to feed me more.'

'Of course. She was a lovely woman, but you needed a healthier diet,' Fwl said defensively.

'For six months straight, all that was put on my plate were green vegetables! Broccoli, peas, cabbage, leek! Imagine a diet like that!' Mavis snapped. She put her hand on her hip. 'Leeks for six months! I can't look at a leek to this day without feeling sick.'

'Okay,' he said slowly. 'I see now that I should have been more specific with Mrs Joyce.'

'Not just Mrs Joyce,' Mavis said, turning to Seren. 'When I was nine, I was staying with Mrs Jones. He told her I needed more fresh air.' She turned back to Fwl. 'Do you know what she did?'

'Umm, no.' Fwl chewed his lip.

'She made me live in the back garden. And not just me; she moved the entire contents of her house outside. We lived out there until she died and you shipped me off to someone else.'

Mavis took another deep breath.

'Sit down and try to calm yourself,' Seren said.

Mavis looked at her, nodded, and eased herself onto a rock. She looked up at Fwl. 'You always said it was good intentions. You always said you cared, but you always messed it up.'

'Why didn't you tell me this at the time? Why didn't you say, "Can you ask Mrs Joyce to feed me something else?" I would have changed it.'

'I didn't see you for months on end sometimes, and when I did, you were more interested in what was happening around me. Never interested in what was happening with me.'

'Is that why you're getting involved with the Dewin? Because of what happened to you?' Fwl asked.

'Not because of what happened with me but what happened to *them*. The old women that took me in drove themselves mad trying to make sure I got green vegetables or fresh air. It became an obsession with them. But you didn't see the effects your whispering had on them. I did, and it was hard to watch, I can tell you,' she spat.

Fwl slowly lowered himself to the ground and sat facing her. 'Mavis, I am truly sorry for everything I did to you, whether it was directly or indirectly, but when I guide people, they do not become obsessed. I'm not sure why this happened to the women who took you in, but I promise I'll try and find out.'

Fwl reached out to touch her shoulder but missed as she stood up and brushed herself down. For a moment, Fwl thought he might be getting through to her. He finally understood why she would want to expose the gods, but what she said wasn't true. Her guardians didn't become obsessed. They were just older women, and that's the kind of stuff they do.

'I'll harness the sheep,' Mavis said to Seren. 'You can help the fool.'

'His name is Fred!' snapped Seren. 'And *his* name'—she pointed at Fwl—'is Fwl, not the fool'.

Mavis huffed and approached Fred. 'Here, boy,' she said sternly.

Seren wanted to shout at her for being so stern with Fred, but she didn't have a couple of hours spare to encourage him into the harness. Mavis doesn't seem to care if she hurt his feelings.

I'll apologise to him later and give him extra sugar cubes.

Fred was staring at her. 'Sorry,' she mouthed.

The journey to The Bryn was quiet, except for one incident where Fwl had some trouble with his new body. They had to pull over for him to scramble to the grass. He lay on the floor in a fetal position, wrapping his arms around his middle.

Seren knelt beside him, concern clouding her face.

'I'm dying!' he groaned.

She examined him, trying to narrow down the possible causes of the pain.

'Maybe he's eaten something funny?' Mavis said, watching from the cart.

'He's eaten the same as us. I'm feeling okay.'

'Me too.' Mavis shrugged.

'Maybe it's something more serious, like appendicitis?'

Seren and Mavis eliminated all sorts of medical diagnoses until Seren clicked her fingers.

'He needs the toilet!'

Mavis burst into hysterics and explained to him what was wrong, as his face reddened. Seren sat back on the cart for that conversation. There was no way she was going to explain to him how a bowel movement worked.

After Mavis had sent Fwl into the trees with instructions, she climbed onto the cart, still laughing.

A few moments later, he shouted, 'Mavis!' She howled in a new fit of hysterics.

Fwl sloped out of the trees and slowly climbed onto the cart. He looked at Seren and shook his head.

'Are you feeling better?' she asked.

'Yes, but let's not talk about this again,' he said, turning away from her.

'Agreed.'

The trio reached The Bryn late in the afternoon. They stopped outside a tavern.

'You wait here with Fred,' Seren said to Mavis. 'I'll go in and ask where the stables are.'

Mavis nodded lazily, eyes closed.

'I'll come in with you, Seren,' Fwl said.

Seren looked at Mavis, nodding off in the back of the cart. 'Please look after Fred, Mavis.' She banged the side of the cart with her fist.

'Yes, girl,' Mavis said, opening her eyes slightly.

Fwl waved away her concerns. 'She'll be fine.'

'But will Fred?' Seren said.

'Mavis won't let anything happen to him,' he said confidently. 'I once watched her wrestle two men after they threatened her pet frog.' He chuckled at the memory. 'She acts like she doesn't care, but she does.'

'A pet frog?' Seren said, amused.

'Oh, yes. He ran away in the end, or hopped away, but she cared for him while he was with her.'

Seren and Fwl entered the tavern and walked to the bar. Seren avoided eye contact with the punters, but Fwl greeted them all with a smile and a 'good evening'.

'Ah, good evening, tender,' he said as he reached the bar.

The tender glanced up briefly then continued with his work. Seren and Fwl watched him, fascinated. Like all tenders, he had eight arms, each engaged in a task. Washing glasses, pouring drinks, taking payment. The tender had a trunk instead of a nose, and this was also busy.

'Wonderful creatures,' Fwl said, watching him in awe.

'Excuse me, tender,' said Seren.

'What can I get you?' he asked.

'Would you tell us where the stables are?'

'I'm not the information desk,' he said as his hands swooshed past their faces, much to Fwl's amusement. Seren was used to the way tenders worked. Her father had spent many a night in their local tavern. She had to wait outside, but she would regularly peek through the window to watch the occupants, more out of boredom than curiosity.

He smirked. 'If you buy a drink, I'll tell you.'

'Lovely. I'll have a pint of your best ale, please,' said Fwl, leaning his elbow on the bar.

The tender poured Fwl's drink with one hand and held out another for payment. 'That will be two gold coins.'

Fwl blinked at the tender and turned to Seren.

'Here.' She put her hand in her pocket, pulled out a couple of coins and passed them to the tender. He took them quickly and passed Fwl his pint with another arm.

'Thank you, tender. And Seren,' he said, admiring his pint.

'Is this your first drink of ale?' Seren asked.

'Yes.' He held up the glass. 'I've always wondered what it would taste like.'

He lifted the pint with one hand and gulped it down in one go.

'I don't think you should have done that,' Seren gasped. 'It'll go straight to your head.'

Fwl planted the empty glass on the bar. 'Another please, tender!' he shouted.

Before Seren could object, the tender poured another pint while gesturing for payment.

She frowned at the tender. 'That's the last one. Don't give him any more,' she said, passing him two more gold coins.

Fwl lifted the pint and drank it in one go. Some ale squirted from his mouth and onto the bar. The tender jumped straight into action and snorted it up with his trunk.

'And that's why you're the tender,' shouted Fwl. 'Did you see that, Seren? He's doing the job of five people. Truly amazing creatures.'

Seren turned back to the tender. 'Please, where are the stables?'

'We've got a cheap to stable, um a sheepy to put in the stable?' Fwl slurred. 'A sheepy, name's Fred.' He smiled at Seren.

'A sheep?' asked the tender.

'Yes, a little sheepy called Fred,' Fwl repeated.

'You can't put a sheep in the stables,' the tender said.

'And why not?' said Fwl, slamming his fist on the bar. 'My gold coins are as good as the next man's, are they not? Well, her gold coins. I don't actually have any gold coins.' He slapped the bar with his hand again. 'Ow, that hurt.' He rubbed his palm.

Seren looked at the tender with pleading eyes. 'Which direction?'

'Through the doors, turn left, down to the end of the road and turn right,' replied the tender.

'Thank you so much.' Seren turned to leave. 'Fwl? Where did he go?'

'Over there,' said the tender, pointing with one of his hands.

Fwl was running from table to table, drinking dregs of ale from empty glasses.

'Fwl!' she snapped. 'Stop that at once. It's disgusting!'

She ran over and grabbed his arm. 'You can't do that,' she said as she marched him out of the tavern.

'Why not?' he retorted childishly.

'First of all, it's disgusting drinking out of someone else's glass. Secondly, you've never had ale before so you're not used to it. You'll make yourself ill.'

They walked to the cart to find Mavis sleeping.

'Mavis!' Seren shouted. 'You said you would look after him.'

'He still there, isn't he?' Mavis said, stretching.

'Yes, but you weren't watching him. You were sleeping,' Seren snapped.

'Nope, girl, I was resting my eyes. I was awake. Don't worry. Nothing would have happened to him,' Mavis said.

Seren kneeled in front of Fred to make sure he was okay. 'He's drunk,' she stated.

Mavis shot up. 'What? How can he be drunk? He hasn't moved.'

'Not Fred,' Seren said. 'Fwl.'

Mavis turned to Fwl who was swaying on the spot, a big grin plastered across his face. 'I'm shlightly tipshy, not drunk.'

'How long were you in there? How long have I been sleeping?' Mavis said, looking confused.

'So, you *were* sleeping?' Seren remarked.

Seren moved away from Fred, but her eyes didn't leave Mavis.

'Ah, not now, girl, poor Fwl is drunk,' Mavis said. 'Did you find out where the barn was?'

'Yes, down the end of the road and turn right.'

'Let's get this poor chap on the cart,' said Mavis, giving Seren a sideways glance, no doubt to see if there was any anger in her expression.

'Come on, Fwl.' Mavis grabbed his arm and led him towards the cart. 'Put your foot up on there.' She patted the step.

Fwl lifted his leg and it hovered in the air for a few seconds.

'I don't think I can,' he said.

'Just put it there,' Mavis said, patting the step again.

Fwl looked down to see where she was patting and lost his balance.

He fell backwards with a shout and thudded on the ground.

Mavis stood over him and sighed. She turned to Seren who was still fussing over Fred. 'You'll have to give me a hand with this one. He's a mess.'

Once they had put Fwl in the cart, they made their way to the stables. They found it without any problems, except for when Fwl fell out of the cart. Twice.

'You can't put a sheep in the barn,' the stable hand shouted at Seren.

She's a kind girl, Mavis thought, as she watched Seren plead with the young man. The lengths she went to for that sheep were truly remarkable.

'But he won't be any trouble,' Seren said.

'It's not him I'm worried about. The horses won't like it.'

Mavis turned to Fwl who was leaning back and sleeping with his mouth wide open. *He's such an idiot.*

Seren approached. 'He won't let Fred in the barn with the horses but he's letting him stay in the old shed. Apparently, it's big enough.'

'Well, yes, a shed would be big enough for a sheep,' Mavis said, frowning.

'I mean it's big enough for all of us,' Seren said.

Mavis put her hands on her hips. 'What? I thought we were going to find a room for the night. You know, one with a comfy *bed*.'

'What gave you that idea?'

'Because we're in a village, not out in the forest. That's what people do. They get rooms!' Mavis shouted. 'Wait, would you have stayed in the barn with the horses if Fred was allowed?'

'Of course. I'm not going to leave him on his own,' Seren said.

Mavis elbowed Fwl. 'Wake up and listen to this.'

'Wha—' he groaned.

'She thinks we're sleeping in a shed tonight,' Mavis said.

'That sounds lovely, Seren,' he said sluggishly.

'Come on, the shed is behind the barn. We can leave the cart here.'

Seren unhooked Fred and practically dragged him to the shed.

'This is wonderful, Seren. They've even got, umm, hay on the ground. Better than the floresht floor.' He leaned into Seren and chuckled.

'Still drunk, clearly. Dip your head in that bucket of water.' Mavis said dryly, pointing at the bucket. 'It might sober you up.'

The shed was just about large enough. Four wooden walls and a roof were all they needed … apparently. Mavis disagreed with Seren on this, but she didn't have her own gold coins to get a room to herself.

'I'm exhausted,' Seren said as she pulled a candle out of her bag and lit it. 'It's taking so long to reach the south.'

She placed the candle on a small wooden box.

'I know you're concerned about your brother, girl. But it's no good worrying about something you have no control over.'

'That's easier said than done,' Seren said. She watched as Mavis brushed clumps of hay together to make her bed a little comfier. Simon's face slid into her mind. What if he'd been sentenced and she hadn't been there to show her support?

Seren turned to see Fwl holding the candle, looking deep into the flames. She realised it was the first time he'd held a candle. What's more, he was swaying.

'I think you should put that down very carefully. Mavis, could you come here for a moment? Slowly and quietly, please.'

Mavis walked over to Seren, looking confused. 'What did—.' She saw Fwl. 'Ah, put that down and come and have a chat with me.'

'Look how pretty it is.' He lifted the candle up higher.

'Yes, very pretty.' Mavis looked at Seren and shrugged.

'Fwl, I need you to come and help me, please,' Mavis said.

He turned to her. 'Of course I will.' He walked towards her, then stopped. 'Wait, I

140

forgot my bag.' As he turned around, the candle slipped off its holder and landed in the dry hay.

Mavis shrieked and grabbed a blanket. Seren snatched up the bucket of water. They both went wild trying to stomp out the flames, but nothing could be done. The fire ripped through the hay and started to climb the sides of the shed.

'I'll grab Fred and you grab him,' Seren shouted.

Mavis grasped Fwl's arms and pulled him towards the door. 'Come on, you fool. Run!'

Once outside, they observed the carnage. First, the shed went up in flames, then all three houses next to it.

The occupants ran out and stood, helpless, in their night clothes.

The stable hand sprinted towards the trio. 'What did you do?' he shouted, holding his hands on his head.

'We didn't do anything,' Mavis snapped defensively.

He pointed angrily. 'You've burned the shed and those houses!'

'That wasn't us.' Mavis folded her arms across her chest.

'I think it was me, wasn't it?' Fwl said.

Mavis dropped her arms and looked at him with disdain.

'Constable, arrest that man!' the stable hand shouted, pointing at Fwl.

'You could have kept your mouth shut,' Mavis said.

'Wait!' Seren yelled. 'It was an accident. He didn't do it on purpose.'

The constable rushed up and grabbed Fwl, putting his hands behind his back. 'You're nicked, pal.' He marched him off.

'Where are you taking him?' Seren shouted.

'To the nick,' the constable called over his shoulder.

Seren stared in disbelief. Mavis stood laughing.

'What's funny?' Seren snapped.

'He's just been arrested,' Mavis said, looking confused as to why Seren wasn't finding it amusing.

Seren rubbed her hands down her face. 'I can't believe this is happening.'

'I did tell you, girl. Your life is going to get a lot harder because of him,' Mavis said.

'You can't see him. He's being processed,' the constable said.

Seren and Mavis had just arrived at the
police station with Fred, all three hot from
running.

'How long will that take?' asked Seren.

'As long as it takes,' he snapped.

The two women sat on the steps outside
the station. Fred dozed off beside them.

Seren peered at Mavis out of the corner
of her eye. 'Why don't you like him?'

'Who?' replied Mavis.

'Fwl. You don't like him. I know you think
he controls people, but he doesn't seem a
bad person.'

'You haven't known him long, girl,' said
Mavis. 'He thinks everything is fine and
dandy. I used to tell him all the time that it
wasn't. He'd say, "Don't be silly, Mavis," then
brush past my concerns. He never listened to
me.'

'What will the Dewin do?' Seren asked.

'I don't know, but they promised to show
the people of Hiraeth the truth. And that's
what I want. I've watched too many people
go crazy because of him. I want it stopped,'
Mavis said

'What do you think will happen to him
once the Dewin have exposed him?'

'I don't know.'

Seren was upset over Mavis's lack of empathy towards Fwl. Mavis had known him since she was born, but to expose him without knowing what would happen to him seemed cruel.

Fwl came flying through the station doors. 'Ladies, I have been let out on something called "dale"? And I have been summoned to a court hearing tomorrow morning,' he said, beaming.

'It's "bail". And that's nothing to smile about, you fool.'

'We need to get out of here before you end up in jail,' Seren said.

Fwl's face dropped. 'Jail? They didn't say anything about jail.'

'What do you think the court hearing's for?' Mavis asked.

'I don't know … but I'm starting to feel a little funny.' He clutched his stomach.

'What do you mean?' Seren asked.

'Well, my head feels bad, and my stomach feels … um, kind of swirly.'

'Swirly?' repeated Seren.

'Ye—' He turned and threw up over the steps.

'It's called a hangover,' Mavis said, then started laughing uncontrollably.

144

Owain was sat in his office, shuffling through paperwork, when there was a knock on the door.

'Enter.'

'There's someone to see you,' the guard said.

Owain gathered the paperwork and placed it in the desk drawer.

'Show them in.'

The guard stood to one side to let the visitor pass.

Owain looked up. 'Ah, Anna. Any news?'

Anna was a god of Gwyn. One of the watchers. As she cautiously stepped inside, her eyes darted around the room. Her hands were trembling slightly, and she clasped them together.

The security guard closed the door quickly.

'Yes, sir. I've come with a report.'

'Excellent.'

'He got drunk on ale. He burned down one shed and three houses. He got arrested by the local constable. He has broken a court summons. And um ...' she hesitated. 'He vomited on the steps of the police station.'

'That's a lot in one day, don't you think, Anna?' Owain asked.

'Yes, sir.'

'And what is he doing now?'

He's making his way out of The Bryn with a hangover, sir.'

'Was there anything else?' he asked.

'Not yet, sir.'

'Thank you for bringing me the report. You may continue your observations.'

'Thank you, sir.' Anna gave a little bow and rushed from the room.

Once she had left, Owain got up and walked to the window. 'Do you still believe the plan will work?'

'Yes,' came the reply.

DRAGONS AND WITCHES

'What does that sign say, Seren?' Fwl asked from the back of the cart.

'Keep off the grass,' she read out loud.

'I wonder why they don't want us t—' Fwl gasped as the field came into view.

'Dragon!' he said, pointing excitedly.

Seren and Mavis followed his gaze and were met with the most beautiful sight Seren had ever seen. An enormous red dragon, with maroon spines running down its back. Standing tall and proud a majestical creature. Its scales shimmering in the sunlight. A rope was around his neck, the other end held securely by a trainer.

Mavis grabbed hold of Seren's arm. 'Before you do anything silly, girl, I want to remind you that it's a dragon.'

'I wasn't going to. Like what, anyway?' Seren brushed Mavis's hand away and slowed the cart to a stop. 'But now that you mention it, I've never seen one up close.' She climbed off the cart.

'Wonderful creatures,' said Fwl. 'So graceful and intelligent.'

The dragon's head snapped in their direction. He saw the trio and started to run towards them, not in an aggressive I'm-going-to-eat-you kind of way, but more of an I'm-excited-to-see-you kind of way.

This particular dragon seemed clumsy, tripping over his feet as he ran towards them. He stood up, shook his head and started to run again. His trainer was holding onto the rope for dear life, his feet desperately trying to catch up with the rest of his body. They failed, and he fell flat on his face, still holding on to the rope as he was dragged through the field face down.

Seren's excitement mounted. The closer the dragon got, the wider her smile became. 'Look at him. He's adorable.'

Mavis could see the danger. If that dragon didn't stop in time, he could do some serious damage to all three of them. As he got closer and faster, panic set in for Mavis.

'Move out of the way, girl. He's not stopping,' she shouted.

She grabbed Seren's shoulders and pushed her up the road, but the dragon changed direction and ran at them.

Mavis looked at Fwl, who was grinning from ear to ear. 'Have you forgotten?' she shouted.

'Forgotten what?' he said.

'YOU'RE HUMAN!'

Fwl's face dropped and lost all colour. 'What do I do?'

'Run, you fool!'

He darted away and dived through a hedge into the next field.

'Stop him!' Mavis shouted to the dragon's trainer, still being dragged behind the beast.

He looked up with a face covered in dirt. 'Where's your toy?' he shouted.

The dragon stopped dead in his tracks and turned to the trainer. He hopped from foot to foot in excitement.

'Aww, look how cute he is,' said Seren, beaming.

Mavis glanced at her. 'Yeah, adorable.' She rolled her eyes.

'He could have crushed us, you know,' Mavis said to the trainer.

'Don't be silly, Mavis, he would never hurt us,' said Seren, climbing over the fence to get closer to the dragon.

'Sit, Jasper!' the trainer shouted and pulled out a toy ball from his bag.

Jasper did as he was told. He lifted his front paw and waited patiently … for all of two seconds, then he nudged the trainer so hard with his snout, the man went flying and landed a few feet from Mavis.

Mavis looked down at him. 'You're doing a great job with him, boyo,' she said and chuckled.

Jasper stood and ran towards the trainer, who quickly threw the ball from his position on the ground. Jasper ran after it. Once he had caught it in his mouth, he looked around to see if everyone had seen his amazing catch.

'Well done, Jasper!' shouted Seren, as she was desperately trying to get closer to him. 'Where's your toy?' she shouted.

Jasper ran towards her and dropped the ball at her feet. She quickly picked it up and threw it, clearly having learnt from the trainer's mistake.

The trainer got up and slowly rubbed himself down. 'He's going to be the death of me,' he said.

'He doesn't seem to be like other dragons,' Fwl said, poking his head up from his hiding place behind the bushes.

'No,' said the trainer. 'He's *very* different. No matter what I do or how he's trained, it never seems to stick in there.' He jabbed at his head with his finger. 'He's untrainable. I just take him out for walks, you know, to make sure he gets his exercise, but he's hard work.'

'Catch!' shouted Seren. 'Good boy!' She clapped her hands, which seemed to excite Jasper even more, and his tail wagged faster.

The trainer gestured to her with his thumb. 'There's no fear in her, is there?'

'Ah, no, our Seren isn't scared of animals,' said Fwl, giggling.

Mavis tutted. 'She should have been scared of that thing running towards her like that. Honestly, she thinks all animals are kind and they don't want to cause harm. She's a danger to herself, that one.' She watched Seren running around with Jasper in the field.

'Come on, girl,' Mavis shouted.

'Can we stay a little longer?' Seren pleaded.

'We don't have time to waste, girl. Come on.'

'Let her stay a little longer. Look how happy she is,' said Fwl.

'I know why you're dragging your feet, but she's got her brother to deal with,' Mavis snapped.

'Are you her parents?' asked the trainer.

Fwl started giggling.

'Don't be ridiculous,' Mavis snapped. 'He's old enough to be my great-great-great-great, or something, grandfather.'

The trainer looked confused.

'It's a long story and I don't have time to explain,' she said. 'Girl, let's go!'

Seren threw the ball for Jasper one last time.

'We could have stayed a little longer, Mavis,' Seren said once they were safely back in the cart.

'That's what I told her, but she wouldn't listen,' Fwl said, folding his arms. Mavis always had to run the show.

'Girl, you need to see to your brother, and I've got my own thing to do,' Mavis said. 'We're running out of time.'

'Not really,' said Fwl from the back of the cart. 'You can take your time, Mavis. You don't *need* to go anywhere.'

Mavis ignored him and sat in silence.

Fwl noticed a bag in the back of the cart that he'd never seen before. He picked it up and examined it. There was something very large and round inside. He opened the bag and pulled out a large ball.

Thundering footsteps pounded from behind. Fwl turned to see Jasper running flat out in the field right beside them.

'Oh my god!' shouted Mavis. 'Throw it, you fool!'

Fwl faced Mavis with a blank stare. 'There's no need for language like that,' he said calmly.

There was an almighty roar. Fwl turned his head so fast, he nearly snapped it. He saw Jasper at the edge of the field slowly lifting his head, and a deep roar emerged from his throat. He opened his mouth wide and flames shot out. Mavis pushed Seren sideways off the cart and jumped on top of her.

'Jump, Fwl!' Mavis screamed.

Fwl leapt out just in time. The fireball blasted the cart into the air, and it landed on its side. The flames took hold.

Seren rushed to the cart. 'Fred! Get him off, get him off!' she screamed.

Mavis and Seren quickly unhooked the sheep. Seren picked him up and ran away from the burning cart. Fred appeared to be unharmed.

153

Fwl landed at the side of the cart and was now lying flat on his back when Mavis cried, 'Fwl, grab my bag! Grab it!'

Through his confusion, he heard her huff and climb onto the burning cart for her bag. He pushed himself up just as she screamed and he saw that the flames had reached her arm. She fell backwards and landed near him.

He scrambled to his feet and rushed to her side. 'Why did you do that, Mavis? You could have died!'

'Don't be silly; I had plenty of time.' She got up and brushed herself down.

'You've burned your arm.'

Mavis held up her arm. 'It's just a graze.'

'A graze?' he said, horrified. 'Your skin has melted.'

Seren ran over to where they stood, Fred still in her arms. He was struggling desperately, his eyes nearly popping out of his head, but Seren held on with the strength of twenty men.

'Are you okay, Mavis?' Seren quickly asked. 'Look at the state of your arm!'

'It's fine. I'm fine,' Mavis said, batting away her concern.

Seren and Fwl glanced at each other.

'I think you should put him down before his eyes jump out, girl,' Mavis said, pointing at Fred.

'Huh?' Oh, yeah.' Seren slowly bent down to make sure his feet touched the ground before letting him go. 'There, there, Fred,' she said. 'You're safe now.'

She kept hold of the harness, knowing full well that if she let go, he would run off, and she didn't have time to chase him. Not now they have no cart. The flames had burned hers beyond repair.

The dragon trainer caught up with Jasper at the edge of the field and climbed over the fence.

'What happened?' he asked, eyes wide in shock.

'What happened?' repeated Mavis, raising her voice. 'That beast of yours burned our cart!' She jabbed a finger at the charred wood.

He clasped a hand to his head. 'I'm so sorry. He's never done anything like that before.' He turned to Jasper who seemed happy standing at the edge of the field, watching the flames.

'This fool picked up your bag,' Mavis said, gesturing at Fwl.

'I didn't know it was his bag,' he said, pouting.

'Then he looked in the bag and pulled out the ball,' she snapped. 'I told you to throw it! But you just held it, looked stupidly at it.'

'Well, I didn't know what it was at first,' he said. 'It all happened so fast.' Fwl slowly crouched on the ground. 'So fast.' He held his head in his hands.

'You're hurt,' the trainer said, pointing at Mavis's arm.

'It's fine,' she said.

'Maybe she's in shock and can't feel it?' Seren suggested.

'I can feel it just fine, girl,' Mavis snapped. Seren looked around to find Mavis a spot to sit down.

'Here,' said Seren, reaching out to hold on to Mavis. 'Sit by this tree.' She guided Mavis to the spot and helped her down. 'Lean against the tree and rest for a while.' Seren turned to the trainer. 'Do you have anything for that burn?'

'Yes, all trainers keep ointment, you know, for the burns we get quite regularly, but I've never seen him do that.' He looked at Jasper in the field and shouted, 'Naughty boy!'

'Don't shout at him. I'm sure he didn't mean it,' Seren said.

Fwl and Mavis gave each other a quick glance while the trainer rooted around in a satchel for the ointment. He pulled out a bottle and bandage and knelt next to Mavis.

'I'm going to put this on and wrap your arm in this bandage. I have to warn you: it's going to be painful for a few seconds, then you won't feel it at all,' he said.

'Right, okay, just put it on,' Mavis said.

He opened the bottle and poured the ointment onto her arm, then waited for the scream. It never came. He looked at Mavis, then he lifted the bottle to eye level and peered at the content inside. He looked back at Mavis. 'Doesn't that hurt?'

'No,' she huffed.

The trainer looked impressed and continued to tend to her wound.

'How long should she keep that on for?' asked Seren.

'A couple of days. Keep it dry,' he said.

'Did you hear that, Mavis?' Seren said, raising her voice a little and patting her companion's shoulder.

'I burned my arm, girl; I didn't go deaf. Why you shouting?'

Once the trainer had finished dressing Mavis's arm, Seren stood up to assess the situation. 'So, we've got no cart, no food and no water.'

'Mmm,' said Fwl, looking sheepish.

'Where's the nearest village?' Seren asked the trainer.

'That would be Armford. It's that way, but it'll take you a few hours to get there,' he said, looking at the charred remains of Seren's cart.

The trainer packed away the ointment, said his goodbyes and headed towards Jasper.

The travelling trio set off on foot towards Armford.

'How's your arm, Mavis?' Fwl asked.

'It's going to be a long walk. Let's save our energy for that.'

'What does that mean?' he asked, looking at Seren.

'She's telling you to shut up,' Seren said, laughing.

'Look,' Fwl said, pointing ahead. 'Smoke. That's got to be a campfire, right? Let's go down there; they may have food and water.' He skipped down the hill.

'We can't just walk over to someone and expect them to feed us, Fwl,' Mavis shouted after him. 'They could be bandits or worse.'

Fwl slowed his pace and fell back in step with the women.

'I think we should get closer to see who they are first before walking into their camp.' Seren said to Fwl. 'Keep your head down.'

'Of course, safety first,' he said, walking towards the smoke.

The trio crept closer to the smoke-filled area and crouched behind a cluster of bushes. All three poked out their heads. A small fire was hosting a huge cooking pot, tended by a woman who looked fairly old.

'Poor, lonely woman,' Fwl said. 'She might want some company.

'I think we should leave,' Seren whispered.

'Leave?' Fwl whispered back.

'Yeah, she's right. Let's go,' Mavis said.

The smell of the food cooking made Fwl's belly rumble. He jumped up quickly.

'Hello there,' he said with a smile and a small wave.

'Fwl,' snapped Mavis.

The old woman stopped stirring the contents of the pot and turned slowly to face him.

He held his hand to his chest and shot her a friendly smile. 'My name is Fwl,' he said, slowly walking forwards. 'We have been walking for hours and we're parched. These are my friends.' He gestured to Mavis and Seren. 'We had a slight accident with our cart and um … we lost it.'

'Lost it?' repeated the old woman. 'And the horse?'

Fwl looked slightly confused. 'What horse?'

'The one pulling the cart,' the old woman said.

'Oh, no, we have a sheep that pulls the cart,' he said, gesturing to Fred.

The old woman shot her eyes at Fred.

Seren instinctively took a sidestep to shield him from her gaze. 'His name is Fred.'

'Fwl,' Mavis whispered, 'I think we should leave.'

He ignored her and extended his outstretched hands to the old woman. 'I can see you have a large pot on the fire. I was wondering if we could join you for a spot of lunch, please.'

The woman peered at him without a word.

'Would there be any spare cawl? We won't take much, honestly.'

'Fwl?' interrupted Mavis.

He inclined his head in her direction. 'Mavis, I'm more of a people person than you are, so let me do the talking. *Please*.'

He returned his attention to the woman by the fire. 'Um, as I was saying, we've been—'

'Take a seat,' interrupted the old lady, gesturing to three chairs that looked like they were carved out of tree stumps. Fwl was sure they weren't there just now. Or were they?

'Fantastic, thank you so much.' He sat in one of the chairs and stroked a finger along the wood. 'These are wonderful. Did you craft them yourself?'

'I did,' the old woman said slowly.

'Thank you again,' Fwl said. 'What a pleasant surprise to bump into you when we were in such dire need of food and water.'

He turned to Mavis and Seren who were still standing in the same spot and waved them over. 'Come and sit down.'

161

'Um, Fwl,' said Seren. 'I think we should be going.'

'Going? We need to eat and rest, Seren. We've been walking for hours.' He patted the chair next to him.

'Take a seat,' the old woman said, looking at Mavis and Seren.

'It's very kind of you to help us out like this, with us being complete strangers to you,' Fwl said, smiling at the old woman.

She turned to Mavis and Seren and repeated, 'Take a seat,' in a slightly more insistent tone.

They slowly walked to the tree stumps and sat down. Mavis didn't take her eyes off the old woman.

'Mavis!' whispered Fwl. 'Don't be rude to our hostess.'

She didn't respond.

'This is nice, isn't it?' he said, slapping his hands onto his knees.

'Fwl,' said Mavis.

'Mavis, please,' he said. 'This is the problem with you. We've been walking for hours, we were starving, and all of a sudden we stumbled upon this lovely woman.' He held out his palms to their hostess.
'Honestly, you should try to make friends

more, Mavis, find out about other people, where they come from and what they like and don't like.'

'Fwl,' she said again.

'Come on now, Mavis. It's an opportunity to get to know someone.' He turned to the old woman. 'Don't you agree?'

'Yes,' said the old woman. 'Let's get to know each other.'

'See, Mavis, you need to put yourself out there more.' He turned back to the old woman and looked at all the cooking utensils and pots around her. His eyes rested for a long moment on the very, very large knife next to the cooking ingredients. He cleared his throat, 'You must travel a lot if you need all this equipment.' He looked at the large pot again. 'It's very big, isn't it? How on earth did you manage to carry such a large pot down here?' He looked around for any sign of transportation but found none.

A frown slowly formed on his face as he tried to work something out; it was right there at the edge of his brain, but it wouldn't come to the front of the queue.

He turned to Mavis. She was staring at him, her eyes growing narrower. He turned to Seren, who was staring at the old woman.

He flicked his eyes back to their hostess and noticed her black robe and pointy hat. Realisation kicked in.

'Ah, right.' He slapped his knees. 'Um … I think we should get going. It's getting late.'

'Don't be in such a hurry to leave. You haven't eaten yet.' She glanced at Fred.

The roots of the surrounding trees sprouted from the ground and wrapped themselves around the visitors' shins.

'What's happening?' shouted Fwl, frantically trying to pull his feet loose. 'What are you doing?' The roots crept up his legs, around his body and began to wrap themselves around his neck. 'How dare you! Release us at once!' he demanded.

Mavis and Seren were struggling to get themselves loose. 'Well, you've gone and done it now, haven't you, Fwl?' shouted Mavis.

'Fred, stay close,' Seren said, struggling to catch her breath.

'The more you struggle, the tighter they get,' the old woman said, grinning from ear to ear.

'What's the sheep's name, *cariad*? Are you one of those people who think that if they name an animal, it can't be eaten?'

164

Seren didn't take her eyes off the old woman as she said through clenched teeth, 'I swear to god, Fwl, to all the gods right now, if she hurts him, I will skin you alive.'

Mavis and Fwl stared at Seren with wide eyes.

Fwl slowly turned to Mavis. 'That was a bit harsh, right?' he whispered.

Mavis ignored him. 'What do you want with us?' she said to the old woman.

'I don't want anything. You're the ones who walked into my camp, so what do *you* want?' she sniggered.

'We don't want anything,' Seren said quickly. 'Just let us go and we'll be on our way.' She seemed to be struggling the hardest against the roots. She was starting to sweat and wheeze as they tightened around her chest.

'Very well. I'll take him off your hands, and you'll be free to go.'

The old woman snatched the rope wrapped around Fred's neck. 'Come on.'

'What do I do?' Seren screamed. 'Help!' she shouted at Fwl and Mavis. 'Help him, please!'

165

Her scream of despair broke Fwl's heart, so he did the only thing that he could; he started crying uncontrollably.

The sound of Seren screaming made Mavis angry, really angry. The type of anger that starts deep in your soul, then grows and grows. The roots struggled to wrap themselves around Mavis's large legs. She lifted up her feet and smashed them down hard on the roots.

'Oi, bitch!' she growled.

Fwl and Seren fell silent.

Mavis shot up from her seat and lunched at the large knife and held it to the witch's throat. 'Drop the rope,' she growled. The witch released her grip and held up her hands. A grin spread across her face as the trees started swaying, and roots were pulled up from the ground.

'You won't get far, *cariad*,' she said and cackled.

Mavis swung her fist and hit the woman flat on the nose, she fell back, out cold.

Mavis ran to Seren and cut her free from the strangling roots. 'You grab Fred; I'll get Fwl. Go, go, go!' She cut Fwl free. 'Run!' she shouted.

'You knocked her out,' he said in disbelief.

'Move, you fool,' Mavis spat.

Fwl ran so fast that, by the time he stopped to catch his breath, he was lost. He looked around the strange forest and a sinking feeling crept into his stomach. His companions were nowhere to be seen.

Seren, Mavis and Fred had been walking in the forest for over an hour, looking for Fwl.

'Fwl! Can you hear me?' shouted Seren.

'Stop shouting, girl. The witch might hear you. I don't think I have the energy to do all that again.'

'Where is he? We've been walking around for ages. He can't have gone further than us, surely,' Seren said.

'Did you see him run?' Mavis asked. 'Before I'd even bent to grab my bag, he was gone. I bet he's made it to Armford already. We should head there before we starve to death here.'

'We can't just leave him, Mavis. He's human now and he'll never survive on his own. He can't even ask anyone for help. How do you think that would sound? "Excuse me but do you mind giving me a hand? I've only been human for two days so I'm not sure how things work." They'd lock him up.'

'That was an amazing impression of him. You even got his facial expressions on point,' said Mavis.

'The last thing I said to him was that I'd skin him alive. We have to find him.' Seren whispered.

Owain sat at his desk, staring into space.

There was a knock at the door and the guard entered. 'There's someone to see you, sir.'

'Send them in.'

Anna walked in, and the guard closed the door behind her.

'I have a report, sir,' Anna said, a little more confidently than the day before.

'Thank you. When you're ready.'

'He met a dragon. He burned the cart they were travelling in. He invited himself for dinner with a witch.'

Owain looked down and sighed. 'Was there anything else?'

'He's a mess, sir. His clothes are ripped, his shoes are torn and he looks filthy.'

'And where is he now?'

'He's curled up in a ball, crying on the ground in the forest, sir.'

Owain sighed. 'Thank you for the report, Anna. You may continue with your observations.'

She turned and left the office.

Owain slowly stood and walked to the window.

'Do not worry,' a voice said.

'I can't help but worry.'

'He will be fine.'

SOCIAL GATHERING

'Seren! Mavis! Fred!' Fwl had been searching for hours. He leaned his head to the side, in case it helped him hear better. Silence.

He was starting to think they had left him there. No, they wouldn't do that. Actually, Mavis would, but he was sure Seren wouldn't leave him. Well, unless Mavis convinced her to go. Fwl shook his head; she wouldn't leave him. But mayb—

Voices murmured through the trees. *People!* He rushed towards the noise. 'Seren? Mavis?' he shouted.

Fwl ran into a clearing, where at least forty figures were dressed in black hooded robes. No one noticed him standing there. He crept back two steps.

'You're late,' said a voice behind him.

He jumped and spun around. A hooded figure was standing there.

'I'm terribly sor—'

'Put this on.' The man threw him a black robe.

'Ah, I can't wear this,' he said apologetically.

'Why not?'

170

'Well, it's not my colour.' He furrowed his brow and pointed at his suit. 'See, I'm in yellow.'

'You call that yellow?'

Fwl looked and realised how filthy and dishevelled his suit was.

'Well, it's normally yellow.' He brushed himself down frantically, blushing.

'Just put it on. We don't have time for messing about. We've got to go.'

'Go? Where?' he asked.

'Ha. You're a funny one, you are.'

The hooded figure pushed him into the clearing to join the others.

'Hello, my name is Fwl,' he said to one of them. 'Have you seen my friends anywhere? One of them is short and slender with brown hair; she's a lovely girl. My other friend is, well, she's the opposite.'

'Your name is Fwl? Who named you "fool"?'

'My name came first, actually,' Fwl said. 'My friends. Have you seen them?'

'No, pal, I haven't seen your friends. You best put that on before we go,' he said, gesturing to the robe in Fwl's hands.

Fwl sighed and tried to put it on, but it was his first time for that kind of garment.

'Would you mind giving me a hand?' he said to the other man. 'I've only been human for two days, so I'm not sure how things work.'

The man stared at Fwl. 'Are you drunk?'

'Oh no, I've recovered from that. What a nightmare that was. Well, not the drinking part, just the hangover part,' Fwl said.

'Just put your arms in the sleeves,' the hooded figure snapped.

The man wandered away to stand somewhere else. Fwl looked at the robe and tried to work it out. Eventually, he managed to put it on, albeit backwards. He puffed with pride at the result of his efforts, then deflated at the thought of Owain popping in to see him. He'd be mortified if Owain saw him dressed in black.

'Right, lads,' said one of the figures. 'You know what to do.'

There was a murmur of agreement.

'We'll stick to the plan. Let's go.'

Fwl was pushed along with the other people. He was squeezed so tightly among them, he couldn't see a way out, so he stopped struggling and allowed himself to be taken along.

They stopped at a rocky clearing, at the centre of which stood a stone altar. On top of the altar were skulls of various animals.

Fwl's eyes bulged. 'What is this place?' he thought out loud.

'Who said that?' asked a hooded figure.

All hoods turned towards him. He slowly raised his hand. 'I'm sorry, I didn't mean to say that out loud.' He smiled weakly, nervously looking around the group. 'I think I've made a mistake. I was looking for, um, my friends and I must have taken a wrong turn.'

The hooded figures stared at him.

'Are you one of us?' a voice asked.

'I don't think so,' Fwl answered slowly.

'Did you take the oath?' said another.

'No, I've only just got here,' he said, shaking his head in confusion.

'This is a secret society. How did you get in?' asked a different voice.

'I walked in,' he said. 'From over there.' He pointed in the direction from which he'd come.

Fwl looked at the hooded figures that were closing in even more tightly around him.

'I think I'll be going now. This was an accident. I didn't mean to join you,' he said, brushing down his robe nervously.

'We can't let you go. This is a secret society,' shouted a voice.

'But you heard him. He was only looking for his friends,' said another.

Fwl was unsure which voice belonged to which hooded figure.

'Yeah, but he ended up here, in this *secret* society. If we let him go, he might tell others, and then it won't be a secret, will it, Martin?'

They all nodded in agreement.

'Honestly, I won't tell anyone about this, um ...' He looked around again. 'I won't tell anyone about this little party of yours.'

'Little party? This is a secret society to celebrate our almighty Lucifer! This isn't a little party,' shouted a voice.

'Bill, what you telling him that for? He just said he wasn't a member,' Martin snapped.

'He called it a little party. It's not a little party,' Bill said.

'My apologies,' Fwl said, lifting his hands defensively. 'I didn't mean to upset anyone.' He shifted on the spot.

'You know, come to think of it, I always thought of it as a party, you know, a sort of get-together with friends,' said one of the hooded figures. Most of them nodded.

'Yeah, a get-together; I like that,' said another.

'Sometimes I'm not even bothered about the devil-worshipping thing. I just come here for the company,' said another.

They all nodded again.

'Shall we just stop, then? You know, with the worshipping, and just meet here every week for a catch-up? It would save all the organising; getting all the skulls ready every week and splattering the fake blood everywhere,' Bill said.

'Fake blood?' repeated Martin. 'I always thought it was real blood.'

'Real blood? Where the hell did you think I was getting real blood from?' asked Bill.

'I don't know,' Martin said, scanning the animal skulls on the altar. 'Animals?'

Bill gasped. 'I'm not a monster!'

Fwl was getting more confused by the second. 'I'm sorry to interrupt, but I need to leave and find my friends. So, I'll just be going that way.' He pointed. He didn't care which direction he pointed in as long as he wasn't here anymore.

'We can't let you leave yet. We haven't decided if we are a secret society or a little party,' said Bill.

'Let's take a vote,' said Martin. 'Who wants it to be a party? All those in favour, say aye.'

'Aye,' they all said in unison.

'Okay, then. We're all in agreement it's a little party,' Bill said and pulled down his hood. 'No more skulls or fake blood. Happy days. Who fancies a drink?'

Fwl stood in the clearing, watching the men walk away. He turned to the scene before him. Animal skulls, fake blood, and … who was Lucifer?

He took off the black robe and gently placed it on the altar. After a furtive glance over his shoulder to check they were no longer interested in him, he shot off before they remembered he was there.

'Can you hear that, Mavis?' Seren asked, reaching out to hold her companion's arm.

'Yeah. What is it?' Mavis said.

'I'm not sure. Let's find out.'

'Hang on now, girl. We just escaped a situation that we went to "find out" about and ended up face to face with a witch. How do we know it's safe?' Mavis asked.

'We don't know but we can't stay in this forest, walking around in circles. Fwl might be with whatever that noise is,' Seren said.

'Or he could be the reason for the noise,' Mavis muttered to herself.

'I heard that,' Seren snapped. 'Let's just get a little closer and try to work out what it is, then we can make a decision.'

Seren and Mavis edged closer to the noise and stumbled on a group of women who were walking in the direction of the noise. They wear wearing identical hats that had 'Rock us!' written on them.

'Excuse me!' Seren called.

'What happened to getting closer before making any decisions?' Mavis snapped.

'They might know what the noise is about,' Seren said. 'Excuse me!' she shouted again.

The group of women stopped talking, turned to them and looked them up and down.

One of them said with a frown, 'Can we help you?'

'Could you tell us what that noise is?' Seren asked.

'Noise?' asked the woman, putting her hands on her hips. 'That *noise* is music.'

Mavis scoffed. 'That's not music. That's someone screaming in pain.'

'It's a rock concert,' the woman said, laughing.

'What's a rock concert?' Seren asked.

'It's a bunch of people getting together and playing music on the stage. Its behind the tree line over there.' the woman pointed.

'I'm telling you, that's not music,' Mavis repeated, covering her ears.

The woman laughed again. 'You should come in and watch the show.'

Seren turned to Mavis. 'Shall we go in? Fwl might be in there.'

'If he's stupid enough to go in there with all that noise, he can stay there.' Mavis pointed at Fred. 'We can't take him in either.'

'Come on. Fred will be fine,' Seren said, dragging Mavis by the arm. 'We need to find him.'

'No, we don't,' snapped Mavis, but she let Seren pull her towards the noise.

'We'll show you in,' the woman said. 'There might be a bit of a queue.'

Seren, Mavis and Fred followed the group of women to the end of a line of people outside.

'How long do you think the queue is?' Seren asked.

'About thirty minutes,' the woman said.

'Do you come to this noise—I mean this concert—often?' Mavis said.

The woman chuckled. 'You two are funny.' She pointed at Mavis. 'Is she your mother?'

'I'm nobody's mother! The flipping cheek,' snapped Mavis.

'Sorry,' Seren said to the woman. 'She's like that all the time.'

'That's okay,' the woman replied. 'My grandmother's the same.'

Mavis took a deep breath. Seren could see she was about to pop off at the woman.

'Mavis, don't,' Seren whispered. 'We need to get in and find out if Fwl is there or if he's been there. *Please*.'

Mavis looked at Seren. 'That one's got a cheek.'

'My name is Amy. Nice to meet you.'

'I'm Seren, this is Mavis and that's Fred.'

179

'Yes, and I'm not her mother or grandmother!' Mavis snapped.

'Sorry about that,' Amy said nervously. 'I just assumed, with you being a lot older.' She shrugged her shoulders.

'Do you come to these concerts often?' asked Seren.

'Yes, our husbands have a get-together once a week. They think we don't know about it. It's ridiculous, really. They get together to worship Lucifer, end up getting drunk and crawl home in the early hours. Sometimes they have fake blood all over their clothes.' Amy shook her head. 'I don't know what that's about. I don't bother asking.' She laughed.

'So, while they are there, you come here?' said Seren.

'Yeah, we go out after they leave, and we're home before they get back. It's brilliant.'

The queue moved quickly for a while, then stopped.

'This is the worse part. You think you're on the move, then it grinds to a halt,' Amy said, raising onto her tiptoes to see over the queue.

'What is this place called?' Mavis asked, still clasping her hands to her ears.

'The Tide. It holds rock concerts every week. It's hosted by Leigh and Clare. They're amazing,' Amy said, beaming.

'Never heard of them,' Mavis said.

The crowd moved forward.

'We're nearly there!' Amy squealed in excitement. Seren turned to Mavis to see if that squeal was enough to push her over the edge. No, she was stood still, hands over ears. She gave Seren an eye roll and Seren smiled in return.

Amy pointed to a wooden gate. 'There's the entrance. Once you get in, turn right so you can walk around the crowd.'

Seren and Mavis passed through the wooden gate and saw crowds of women at the centre of a clearing facing a stage, they turned right.

'Go around the edge of the crowd, Mavis!' Seren shouted.

'What?' Mavis yelled back.

Seren gestured with her arms to go around. As they approached the stage, the music became louder. Seren was struggling to see anyone in the dark, and Fred kept walking into people. Seren had to apologise every few seconds.

She turned to talk to Mavis but the old woman had disappeared from her side. Seren's chest fluttered, not because Mavis was lost but because the grouchy woman could say or do anything she wanted. And if someone upset her, she might snap and do something stupid like burn down the concert.

'Mavis!' Seren screamed.

Seren squeezed her way through the packed crowd of women, apologising with every step.

'Mavis!' she shouted. 'Sorry, that was your foot. I didn't see it. Mavis!' She gave Fred's rope a tug. 'Come on, Fred,' Seren shouted, doubting he could hear her.

Seren and Fred walked the length of the concert and back, screaming for Mavis. A commotion caught Seren's eye at the front of the crowd. Her heart sank. It had to be Mavis. She pushed her way through the crowd, only to be met with the most shocking sight she had ever seen. Mavis was at the front, lifting up her blouse and asking the band members to autograph her chest.

'Mavis!' Seren shouted. 'What the hell are you doing?'

The old woman started bouncing up and down in rhythm with the music.

'Look, girl,' Mavis said, holding up her blouse. 'They signed my chest.' She cackled.

'Cover yourself up,' Seren said, pushing Mavis's hand away and letting the blouse drop.

'Come on, girl. Live a little,' Mavis said and started bopping her head up and down.

Seren couldn't believe what she was seeing. Mavis was enjoying herself, without a care in the world. Seren looked at the rock band and gave in. She joined Mavis in the head-bopping.

By the time Seren, Mavis and Fred left the concert, they were worn out, but they'd had so much fun. Mavis was hoarse from shouting and singing.

Seren looked at her and started laughing. Her hair was sweaty and sticking up. The buttons on her blouse were undone, showing her undergarments.

'What?' Mavis asked.

'You're a state,' Seren said.

'You're not so tidy either, girl. Look at yourself.'

They both started laughing.

'Right, come on. Armford is this way,' Mavis said.

'Are we sure he wasn't in there?' Seren asked.

'We looked everywhere, girl. If he had been, we'd have seen him.'

Seren nodded. 'Okay, let's walk to Armford. He might be there already, waiting for us.'

'Probably,' Mavis said. She started humming, and the humming grew louder, until she burst into song and continued all the way to Armford.

Fwl scrambled through the trees and bushes. He was getting more desperate to find Seren and Mavis with each step. His clothes were torn, dirty and beyond repair. His shoes had holes in them. He was devastated and all alone.

He reached Armford and ran to the village square. He scanned the area for his friends. People were busying themselves with their daily routines.

'Mavis! Seren! Fred! Someone please help me. I've lost my friends.' He dropped to his knees.

People turned to look at him. What they saw was a man who looked like he'd been living in the wild for years, far from soap or water. Parents pulled their children away from the spectacle.

'I've got to say, Fwl, in all my years, I've never seen you look like this. You're a mess,' Mavis said behind him.

He gasped and looked over his shoulder. 'Mavis! Seren! Fred!' he said, stumbling to his feet. 'I thought I'd lost you. And I had a strange encounter in the forest.' He ran up to Mavis and gave her the biggest hug.

'Mavis, I was so worried about you.' He hugged her tighter.

He pulled away and looked at her.

'That's the first time I've ever hugged you,' he said. 'Anyone, in fact.'

'And it's the last. Get off,' she said, pushing him away.

He turned to Seren and gave her a big hug. 'What a night!' he said as he squeezed her tight. 'And Fred.' He kneeled to try and give Fred a hug, but Fred wasn't having any of it.

'Look at the state of those shoes,' Mavis said.

He looked down and chuckled. 'They've seen better days.'

'Let's find you a cobbler,' Seren said. 'There must be one here somewhere.' They turned into the main street. 'We need to get you some clothes as well,' she said, eyeing him up and down.

'Fwl,' said Mavis. 'Seren does an amazing impression of you.'

'What?' he said, wrinkling his brow. 'An impression? Of me?'

Mavis laughed. 'It's amazing.'

His eyes lit up. 'Let's hear it, Seren,' he said excitedly.

Seren did the impression and his face dropped. 'I don't know what you're talking about, Mavis. That didn't sound anything like me.'

Seren and Mavis burst out laughing.

Owain sat in his empty office, drumming his fingers on the desk. He knew Anna would be there soon. He wasn't sure about this plan. What would it do to Fwl if he failed?

A knock at the door snapped him out of his thoughts.

'Come in,' he said.

186

'There's someone for you, sir,' the security guard said.

Owain nodded. 'Thank you. Send her in.'

Anna entered and Owain gestured to her to stand in front of his desk.

'You have a report?' he asked.

'Yes, sir,' Anna said. 'He joined a secret society and worshipped someone called Lucifer. He's still a mess, sir. His clothes are torn. And ...'

'Yes?' he said, arching an eyebrow.

Anna cleared her throat. 'He wore black,' she said, shifting in her spot.

'Black?' Owain said, surprised.

'Yes.'

'Where is he now?'

'In Armford. He has been reunited with his companions.'

'Thank you, Anna. You may continue with your observations.'

Once Anna had left, he stood and walked to the window.

'Did you hear that?'

'*Yes,*' said the voice. '*Who is Lucifer?*'

'I don't know. He wore black.' Owain said.

'*Yes, I heard.*'

DID YOU SAY 'WITCH'?

They found the cobbler in no time. Seren stayed outside with Fred.

As Mavis and Fwl entered the cobbler's shop, they were immediately struck by the unusual décor. Mounted animals of various sizes and shapes adorned the walls, their glassy eyes staring down at the newcomers. A large deer's head dominated the far corner, its antlers stretching out impressively. Fwl shot Mavis a look of horror. They turned and saw a snarling wolf and a fierce-looking bear against the wall behind the tall wooden counter.

'Can I help you?' said a deep voice from behind the counter.

'Um, yes, I would like my shoes repaired,' Fwl said. He whispered to Mavis, 'Shall we just leave? All of this is unsettling.'

'Don't be silly; you need them repaired. Look at the state of them,' she said, pointing at his feet.

'Okay, but we shouldn't tell Seren about this.' He nodded towards the deer mounted on the wall.

'Definitely not.'

An old man limped from behind the counter. His weathered face, deep with wrinkles, was framed by wispy grey hair and a beard to match. He stopped in front of them and asked again, 'Can I help you?' He stood at a slight angle, his back hunched.

'Did you do that?' Mavis asked, pointing at the deer's head.

'Ah, no,' he said with a giggle. 'The last cobbler was a hunter, I've never had much liking for it myself. You?'

'Definitely not,' Fwl said, slightly offended. 'I could never.' He covered his mouth with his hands.

The old man turned to Mavis. 'What about you, young lady? Do you hunt much?'

'Only when I have to,' she replied.

The old man beamed and patted her on the shoulder. 'Good for you.' He turned and eased himself into his rocking chair.

'He needs those shoes fixed.' She pointed at Fwl's feet.

The cobbler looked down and his eyes widened.

'Oh dear, those might be beyond repair,' said the cobbler.

'I hope not; they're my favourite shoes. Actually, they're my *only* shoes, come to think of it.' He looked at Mavis. 'I wasn't given any others. I've had these my whole life.'

'That's because you've never needed them. When you're in Hiraeth, you float just above the ground. Your shoes never touch anything,' she said, rolling her eyes.

The old man ignored her strange comment and stood up slowly, reaching his hand to his lower back. 'Old age doesn't come alone, I can tell you.' He leaned on the counter and patted it. 'Pop them up here and I'll take a look.'

Fwl walked over, lifted his leg high and placed his shoe, foot, and all, onto the counter.

Mavis guffawed. 'Fwl, you need to take off your shoes and put them on the counter *without* your foot in it.'

'Oh! Sorry,' he said to the old man. 'I'm new to all this.' He sat in the rocking chair, took off his shoes and placed them on the counter. 'There. Can they be repaired?'

'Come back in an hour. I'll have them sorted,' the cobbler said.

'An hour? But I don't have any others to wear.' He turned to Mavis, hoping she would know what to do. But she just shrugged.

'I've got a spare pair, but it will cost you extra,' said the cobbler.

'How much in total?' asked Mavis.

'Five gold coins.'

'I hope Seren's go enough to cover it, otherwise you'll be walking around barefoot.' Mavis laughed. 'I'll see what she's got.'

Mavis walked out of the shop and Fwl watched her talking to Seren through the window.

'You must have been doing a lot of walking by the look of these shoes,' the cobbler said, examining them.

'Yes, and a lot of running. We were caught off guard by a witch.'

The cobbler dropped Fwl's shoes.

'Oops, butterfingers! I'll grab them for you,' Fwl said, laughing.

'What did you say?' the cobbler said as Fwl handed him the shoes.

'Butterfingers. It means you drop things, or they slip out of your hand.' Fwl looked at the cobbler, who had lost all the colour in his face.

'Are you okay?' Fwl asked.

'What did you say about a witch?' the cobbler whispered.

'Oh, that. Yes, we came across her in the woods. Had a lucky esca—' A bell began to clang. Fwl turned to locate the noise, only to find the cobbler frantically shaking a bell. Fwl crouched and covered his ears.

'What are you doing?' he shouted.

The cobbler opened his door, still ringing the bell. 'Witches!' he bellowed and speed-hobbled onto the street.

Fwl followed him out and was met by Seren and Mavis.

The cobbler ran down the street so fast that Fwl wondered if his limp and bad back had magically disappeared.

'What happened? I only left you in there for two seconds! What did you say to him?' Mavis demanded.

'He was trying to make conversation, so I mentioned … you know … the witch,' Fwl said.

'How on earth did *that* come up in conversation?' growled Mavis.

'Witches! Witches! Witches!' Shouted the cobbler running back up the street.

'He asked me if I'd been walking a lot. I said yes, and that we've been running too … from a witch,' Fwl said, wringing his hands.

Mavis glanced at Seren and back to Fwl; she was red in the face.

'I don't know why you're upset, Mavis. He's just warning the residents of this fine village. It's a good thing that I told him, actually; now they can be alert. She might try to hurt people here.' He nodded emphatically. 'Yes, it's a good thing,' he said, looking at all the residents screaming and running back to their homes.

'Fwl?' said Seren. 'Do you remember the roadblocks in Bridgestart?'

'Of course,' Fwl said.

'Do you remember why we couldn't pass?'

Fwl put a finger to the edge of his mouth. 'They wouldn't let anyone in because there might have been a witch about?' he asked.

'They wouldn't let people in *or out* of Bridgestart,' said Mavis.

Fwl turned back to the emptying street. 'Ah, right, I didn't think of that.'

A young man wearing a pointy hat and navy-blue jacket and trousers climbed onto

193

the wall in the village square. He bellowed, 'Citizens of Armford, please safely and quietly return to your homes and barricade the doors. Our constables are en route to block off the entrance of Armford. Please remain in your homes.'

'What do we do now?' Fwl asked his companions, but they were already running down the street. Fwl chased after them. Something didn't feel right. Something definitely didn't feel right. He stopped running and looked down. 'Wait, wait,' he shouted after them. 'I don't have shoes on!'

Seren dashed back to him. 'We don't have time to find you a pair of shoes. Just run, before they close down the village.' She dragged him by his arm. 'Run!'

As they hurried down the street, Fwl caught sight of something strange. 'Hang on. Look at that,' he said, pointing.

A man was carrying a woman across the road. He set her down on the path next to some children. He patted them on the head and said something out of Fwl's earshot.

'What about it? Mavis asked.

'You know who that is?' Fwl said.

'No, who?' Mavis said, looking confused.

'Ah, you were sleeping,' Fwl said.

194

'Who is he, Fwl?' Seren asked.

'It's Garry.'

'Garry?' asked Mavis.

'The man who saved you, remember?' Fwl asked.

'No, I don't. I was out cold,' Mavis said.

They watched as Garry ran across the road, picked up another woman, threw her over his shoulder and ran to the other side.

'Put me down!' she was shouting.

'What's he doing?' Mavis asked.

'He's just picking people up and moving them around,' Seren said.

'Why do you think he's doing that?' Fwl asked.

'Look what's written on the back of his shirt,' Mavis said. 'Hero.'

'He's saving people who don't need saving,' Fwl said. 'How strange.'

Seren tugged at Fwl's sleeve. 'We need to get out of here before they close the exits.'

'Let's watch a bit longer,' Fwl said eagerly.

'We don't have time for this,' Seren said.

He clapped his hands. 'But it's so strange.'

They stood in silence for a moment, Seren shuffling on the spot, then Fwl waved at the hero across the street. 'Garry!'

'Why did you call him?' Mavis snapped.

'He saved your life. Don't you want to thank him?' Fwl asked.

'Mavis and I were unconscious the whole time, and you were invisible. Don't you think Garry might find it strange we know his name?' Seren said.

'I didn't think of that,' he said.

'He's coming over,' Mavis said.

Garry beamed at them. 'It's okay, ladies. I've got you.'

'What do you mean?' asked Seren.

Garry bent down and flipped her over his shoulder.

'What are you doing?' Fwl heard her shouting. 'Put me down right now!' Garry carried her over the road, with Fred trotting behind, still attached to her by the rope.

Garry gently place Seren on the ground, 'What was the point of that?' she asked.

'I'm saving you,' Garry said, looking confused.

'From what?' Seren demanded.

He frowned. 'There are witches in town.'

'And how does carrying me across the road save me from witches?' she asked.

Garry didn't stay to answer her question and dashed back to Mavis. She waved and Seren could hear her screaming, 'Don't you dare pick me up!' Garry threw Mavis over his shoulder and headed back to Seren. Once Mavis was safely on the ground, Garry said. 'Glad to be of service, ladies.'

'Service? What the hell are you doing? Just picking people up and carrying them around?' Mavis shouted at him.

'I'm saving you,' he repeated. 'I've got to go and help the rest. Stay safe, ladies.'

Seren and Mavis watched as Garry lifted another woman over his shoulder as she shouted, 'Put me down!'

Fwl crossed the road. 'Did you see that?' he asked.

'He's lost his mind,' Mavis said.

'No, I mean ... well, yes, his behaviour does seem a bit strange. But he left me there,' Fwl said, looking hurt. 'He didn't even offer to carry me.'

'And?' asked Mavis.

'It's as if I was invisible to him. I may have needed saving,' Fwl said.

197

'He probably thought you were fully capable of taking care of yourself,' Seren said.

'I'm more capable of looking after myself than he is,' Mavis huffed.

Fwl wasn't an expert in human behaviour, but Garry's behaviour was definitely strange. Gwen had told Fwl that Garry had something called 'social anxiety', but there he was, brave and bold. And why was he so far from his family? Gwen had said she was going to take him back, but he was there in Armford. Seren snapped him out of his thoughts.

'We need to leave before we get stuck here permanently. Let's go this way.' She headed down a narrow lane and her companions quickly followed.

They crept through the lane. As they approached the end, Seren crouched and peered above the wooden fence that ran on either side.

She pointed. 'We can get out that way.'

Mavis looked over the fence at the exit. It was a tiny alleyway that looked like it led into the forest at the edge of Armford. There were fences on both sides and it was very narrow.

'I don't think I'll be able to squeeze myself through there, girl,' Mavis whispered.

'Of course you will,' Fwl hissed back.

Mavis scanned the area again. 'Okay, but if I can't get through, leave me here.' She turned to Seren. 'Go and see to your brother.'

'I'm not leaving you, Mavis,' Seren said. 'Let's try it quickly before anyone comes.'

The trio made a run for the exit. Seren and Fwl sidestepped through the alleyway holding Fred up in the air. They reached the other side and gently lowered a very annoyed looking sheep on the ground. Mavis turned to the side but couldn't take a step. Her belly and bag were in the way.

'Throw the bag to me,' Seren shouted, holding her arms out ready to catch.

'No, girl. I can't throw it that far,' Mavis said, grasping her bag.

Fwl rushed past Seren and back through the alleyway. 'I'll take it.' He tried to lift the bag over his head, but Mavis wouldn't let go of the strap.

'Let it go, Mavis. I'll take it through,' he said.

'No, you fool. I won't fit through with or without the bag. Give it back,' she demanded.

Fwl rushed back to Seren. 'She can't fit through,' he said. 'I don't know what's in that bag, but she won't let it go.'

Seren went back to pull Mavis, but she wouldn't budge.

'Just go,' Mavis said, pushing Seren away. 'Go! Go on.'

'I'm not going,' Seren snapped.

'We don't know how long this village will be in lockdown. It could be days. And where will your brother be, then?' Mavis said.

'Shush, Mavis,' Fwl said from behind Seren. 'Try pulling her again.'

Seren pulled and pulled, but Mavis wouldn't budge. Seren let her go and Mavis moved back. She looked at Seren. 'You need to leave. Now! Before it's too late.'

'I have to stay with her, Seren,' Fwl said pitifully.

Seren and Fred moved out of the way for Fwl to pass. He stood next to Mavis.

'You don't have to stay. Go with her and help her,' Mavis said, waving in Seren's direction.

'I have to stay with you,' Fwl said.

'Why? Because that messenger from the devil told you to?' She rolled her eyes.

'No, because you're my ward!' Fwl snapped. 'And Seren can look after herself,' he added, smiling at Seren.

The guards' voices and footsteps were getting nearer.

'Just go. We'll be fine,' Fwl said.

'*I'll* be fine,' Mavis said. 'I'm not so sure about him. Go! They're getting closer.'

'We'll make our way south when we leave here. We'll find you,' Mavis said hastily and shooed Seren away. She threw her bag over her shoulder. 'Come on, you fool. Let's find out how long we'll be staying here.'

Seren watched as Fwl and Mavis slowly walked away. She could hear them talking.

'We can get a room for the night with the gold coins Seren gave me,' Mavis said.

'Those are for my shoes!' he said.

She gave a dismissive wave. 'You'll be fine without shoes. My back is killing me. I need a proper bed.'

'What? I can't walk around barefoot,' he said desperately.

'I thought I was important to you. Including my back,' she said.

Fwl dropped his head. 'Fine. You can have the coins.'

Seren smiled as she watched them go. Their bickering made her heart swell. She was going to miss them. She turned to Fred. 'Just you and me again.'

Seren and Fred walked through the trees. A man shouted, 'Stop! Who goes there?' She ducked quickly and scanned the area, but couldn't see anything through the trees.

'That's him!' another male voice called.

Fwl screamed a little way off. Seren jumped up and ran back to where she had left Mavis and Fwl. The pair were being dragged off by three constables. One was holding Fwl's arms behind his back and the other two were holding onto Mavis.

'Unhand her this minute!' Fwl shouted. 'How dare you manhandle a lady like that, especially at her age!'

Mavis tried to lift her leg to kick Fwl but couldn't get it high enough. Seren frowned. Simon needed her but so did Mavis and Fwl. She couldn't abandon them here. She knew Fwl wouldn't be able to get himself out of trouble, but she also knew Mavis would get herself into more trouble.

'Stop!' Seren shouted. She ran back through the narrow gap with Fred above her head.

'What are you doing?' Fwl asked. 'You should have left already.'

'Why are you dragging them away?' Seren demanded.

'They saw the witch,' said the cobbler from further down the street. 'He came into my shop and told me about the witch they met.' He pointed at Fwl.

'Yes, but why treat them like that?' Seren asked.

'We need to question them!' snapped the constable.

'You can do that without mistreating them,' she said. 'Let them go. Now. And they'll answer all your questions.'

'That's not how we do things, young lady. We need to take him to the police station,' the constable said, puffing out his chest.

Seren started to panic. Fwl had already jumped bail in The Bryn. If this constable found out, Fwl would definitely end up in jail.

Seren smiled at the constable. 'Sir, please, this is a very confused man. We've been looking after him today.' She turned and smiled at Mavis and Fwl. 'He can sometimes make up little stories in his head.'

'Yes,' Mavis said, thankfully catching on to what Seren was trying to do. 'He's a right nutter, that one.' She nodded at Fwl.

'What?' asked Fwl, looking confused.

'We are his caregivers,' Seren said, looking at Fwl sympathetically.

'Look at the state of him. He can't look after himself,' Mavis added.

'Now, hang on,' Fwl said, trying to stand up straight but failing due to his hands being held behind his back. 'I haven't been human for long. I personally think I'm doing a very good job of looking after myself.'

'See!' Mavis turned to the constable. 'He's nuts.'

The constable looked Fwl up and down. 'The cobbler said he'd been running from the witch; that's why he's in such a state.'

'He wasn't running from the witch. He was running from us,' Seren said. 'He thinks he can look after himself.'

'He told me he met a witch! He said he had a lucky escape,' said the cobbler, marching towards them.

'I see your leg and back are better,' Mavis spat.

'We did meet a witch. Mavis knocked her out cold,' Fwl said proudly.

'Did you hear that? Me? An old woman knocking out a witch? He's clearly lost his mind,' Mavis said.

'I have not lost my mind. You were there, Mavis!' Fwl said.

She frowned. 'I'm sure I would remember if I met a witch.'

'What's happening, Seren?' he asked.

'There, there. We'll get you cleaned up and rested once these kind gentlemen let you go.' Seren gently rubbed Fwl's shoulder. 'You've had a long night and you need some rest.'

Seren looked at the constable. There was a long pause before Mavis broke the silence. 'It's nearly time for his medication. So let us go.' She struggled against the tight hold of the two constables.

'Medication?' Fwl stuttered. 'I don't need medication.'

'Show us his medication and I'll let you go,' the constable said.

'It's in my bag,' Mavis said.

He pulled the bag off her shoulder, opened it and turned it upside down. Out dropped a small bottle. The one that Seren had drunk. The constable shook the bag again and out fell a blanket.

'That's Mrs Thomas's blanket. The one she crocheted for you,' Fwl said, beaming. 'You told me you burned it.'

'That's a different one,' she snapped.

'It's not. I remember it like it was yesterday.' He beamed. 'You always held onto it when you were a little girl.'

'When she was a little girl?' questioned the constable.

'Yes, I would visit her all the time and she would be clinging to it,' said Fwl.

'She's older than you, so how could you have visited her when she was a little girl?' he asked.

'Don't be silly. Mavis isn't older than me.' He started chuckling.

Mavis laughed. 'I don't think we need to convince them he's nuts, girl. He's doing that all by himself.'

The constable eyed Fwl again. 'You look about thirty years old. And she looks …' he hesitated for a moment. 'Well, she loo—'

'I'm going to stop you there,' interrupted Seren. 'You hear what he's saying? He clearly isn't well.'

'So, there wasn't a witch?' the constable asked.

'Definitely not,' Mavis confirmed.

The constable picked up the empty bottle from Mavis's bag.

'You'll need to get a refill. You can't have him running around, scaring people like that.' He handed the bottle to Seren.

'Of course. I'm sorry this started a panic. We'll get him rested for the night,' Seren said.

'Right. Lads, let them go.'

'What about the village?' Seren asked. 'Is it still going into lockdown? Now you've confirmed there wasn't a witch ...' Seren said desperately.

The constable's stern silence was broken by Mavis. 'Come on,' she said. 'We've told you he made up the story.'

'I did no such thing!' declared Fwl.

'Shhh, Fwl,' Seren said, rubbing his shoulder again.

'Well, it does seem pointless now.' The constable looked at Fwl again. 'Make sure he gets his medication.' He turned to his companions. 'Send the men to open up the village. And tell the people it was a ... um ...'

'Misunderstanding,' Seren suggested.

Seren, Mavis, Fwl and Fred stood at the edge of the village, watching the constables walk away.

'I'm sorry,' came a voice behind them. They all turned, except for Fred who didn't seem to care who was talking. 'I didn't realise he was, you know.' The cobbler tapped the side of his head. 'I should have thought about it when he put his foot on the counter without taking off his shoe.' He chuckled to himself.

'I need this refilled,' Mavis said, waggling the empty bottle. 'Anywhere in the village? Maybe the same place you get medication for your back and leg. It seems to have done wonders. Old age doesn't come alone, aye?' she hissed.

'Anyway, I must be off,' he said and limped down the street, holding his back.

'Look at him!' Mavis shouted. 'You could swear we didn't see him run out of his shop like a ten-year-old. Honestly, some people are just looking for attention.'

'I'm still confused as to what all that was about,' Fwl said. 'I did see a witch. We all did. Right?'

'*I* didn't see a witch,' Mavis said, looking puzzled.

208

'Don't do that to him, Mavis. He will think he *has* gone crazy.' Seren laughed. 'Yes, we met a witch. But we couldn't let them know that. So, we pretended you were making it up.'

'You didn't need much help from us to look crazy,' Mavis said. 'You should have asked him to sort out your shoes.'

'Oh, my shoes.' Fwl spun on the spot and started running in the direction of the cobbler. 'Stop! I need my shoes,' he shouted, waving his arms above his head.

Seren watched Fwl running. 'You know, I don't think he chose to stay here with you because he was told to or because you're his ward.'

'What do you mean?' Mavis said.

'He's not your god or anyone's god right now. He's human,' Seren said.

'Don't be silly, girl. It's just a habit to stay with me. He's been my god for sixty-two years,' Mavis said dismissively.

'I think it's more than that.'

Fwl had finished talking to the cobbler and was hurrying back to them.

'You're more than his ward. You're his family. That's why he stayed.'

'Don't be ridiculous, girl. He doesn't know what family is. And neither do I, for that matter,' Mavis snapped.

Fwl reached them. 'He said it will take an hour.' He leaned over and rested his hands on his knees to catch his breath.

'I don't know about you two, but I'm exhausted,' Seren said.

'And me, girl. I'm famished. I feel like we've been running all day,' Mavis said.

Seren looked at Fred, who seemed uninterested in what anyone was doing. 'I think he needs to rest as well,' she said.

Fwl picked up Mavis's blanket. He folded it neatly and handed it to her, then picked up her bag and held it open.

'You've kept it safe.' He smiled. 'You even jumped onto a burning cart to save it.'

Mavis didn't respond; she just placed the blanket in her bag.

'You thought I told her to give you the blanket. Is that why you kept it? Because you thought it was from me?' he asked.

'No, you fool. I knew it was from her. She was different from the other women you put me with.' Mavis snatched the bag from his hand and threw it over her shoulder. 'I keep it because I have fond memories of her.'

Fwl smiled. 'She was kind.'

'Yes, she was,' Mavis said quietly. She turned to Seren. 'Come on, girl. Let's find a shed to sleep in for a few hours.' She glanced sideways at Fwl and smirked.

Owain leaned back in his chair, waiting.

There was a knock on the door and the security guard opened it.

'Just send her in, please,' Owain said, brushing down his tie with his hand.

Anna walked in and walked straight to Owain's desk.

'You have news, Anna?' he said.

'Yes, sir.' She took a deep breath. 'He's still a mess. His clothes are torn, and he's still filthy.'

'Anything else?' he asked.

'He almost caused Armford to go into lockdown,' he added.

'How?' Owain asked.

'He told someone he'd met a witch. They assumed the witch was nearby and planned to close the village,' she said.

'But they didn't?' he asked.

'No, sir. His companions convinced the constable that Fwl was, um, crazy. And that he'd made up the witch story.' She smiled. 'He doesn't have any shoes, either.'

'Anything else?' he asked.

'Yes, sir.' Anna smiled. 'I believe Mavis might be changing her mind.'

Owain raised his eyebrows. 'Fwl is convincing her?'

'Not Fwl, sir. I believe Seren is having an impact on Mavis,' she said. 'She seems to be softening a little. She has grown fond of Seren and is rather protective of her.'

Owain folded his hands together and placed his elbows on the desk. 'Was there anything else?'

'Yes, sir. There was a strange man in Armford that believe he was saving women.' She said frowning.

'How does this have anything to do with Fwl or his companions?' he asked.

'Fwl has met him before. That's what he told Mavis and Seren. Apparently, he is a ward of Gwen. A god of Melyn.' She said shifting on the spot.

'And?'

'Fwl seemed to think that this man, Garry, was behaving strangely. He genuinely seemed confused by his actions.'

'What actions?' Owain asked.

'Well, sir. Garry was picking women up and carrying them to the other side of the road. Believing that he was saving them. But he wasn't, sir. He was just moving them around. He seemed determined to save these women.'

'That does seem strange. Was Fwl concerned?'

'Yes. Concerned and confused. But he had enough to be getting on with, so he just left Garry.'

'Okay. Thank you, Anna. I will speak to Gwen. Was there anything else?'

'No, sir.'

'Thank you, Anna. You may continue with your observations,' he said.

Once the door closed, Owain shot up from his chair and strode to the window.

'Did you hear?' Owain said out loud.

'*Yes,*' said a voice.

'This will be a problem,' Owain stated.

'*Maybe, but the plan will still go ahead.*'

'If Mavis changes her mind, then—'

'*If Mavis changes her mind, the plan will still go ahead. We will just need to inform the Dewin of any changes.*'

'Can they be trusted?' Owain asked.

'Have a little faith, Owain,' said the voice. *'You might want to visit Fwl. Once Mavis is aware of your presence, she may become angry again. Angry enough to continue her journey south to meet the Dewin.'*

'I can't. Fwl will ask about Seren's god again,' Owain said.

'Tell him you still cannot locate them.'

'He'll know something's wrong if I say that again,' Owain said.

'I don't believe so, considering all the problems he has had lately. He might not overthink it,' said the voice.

'You could visit *her*?' suggested Owain.

'I've told you it would not be wise for me to interfere until the task is complete,' the voice said sternly. *'Do you not think I would like to visit her?'*

'Sorry, I didn't mean to imply—'

'Enough. Visit him and make his ward angry,' said the voice.

'Just move the bag over there, you fool,' shouted Mavis. 'There isn't enough room for everything over here.'

Fwl sighed and did as she said. He was too tired to argue.

Mavis and her companions had found a small shed to rest in for a few hours. Seren and Fred had settled down and fallen asleep immediately. This was adding to Mavis's irritability because Seren's snoring felt like a nail trying to imbed itself into Mavis's brain.

'I was just trying to make you a comfortable pillow, Mavis,' Fwl said wearily.

'I don't need one, so stop fussing. Just lie down and go to sleep.' She gestured at Fwl's makeshift bed.

The wind picked up and there was a loud pop.

Fwl closed his lips tight and didn't look up at Owain.

'What was that noise?' Mavis snapped. 'Is your friend here? What's he saying?'

'Hello, Fwl,' Owain said.

Fwl didn't acknowledge him at all.

'I've come to check how everyone is.' Owain turned to look at Seren and his mouth dropped open. 'Is she ill?'

Fwl shook his head slightly without looking at Owain.

'Fwl? Seren seems to be making some unusual noises,' Owain said.

'I know he's here, Fwl. It's no good pretending he isn't,' Mavis spat.

Fwl sighed and stood up. 'She's not ill, Owain. That's the noise she makes when she sleeps.'

They watched Seren who was curled up on a mound of hay, sleeping soundly.

'And she sleeps through that noise?' Owain asked.

'Ah, yes, our Seren can sleep through anything,' Fwl said.

'Mmm. I'm a little alarmed by your attire,' Owain said, looking Fwl up and down. 'And the lack of shoes.'

'They're with the cobbler as we speak. They'll be repaired in no time,' Fwl said happily.

'What does he want?' Mavis snapped. 'Ask him if he's found the girl's god. Or is he useless as well?'

Owain smiled softly at Mavis. Not that she would know, but he didn't dislike her. His job as a god didn't allow him to dislike anyone in Hiraeth.

'Unfortunately, I have not been able to locate Seren's god.' He smiled. 'I will need a few more days.'

'Don't you think it strange, Owain?' Fwl asked, frowning. 'The whole time I've been with her, there hasn't been any sign of a god.

216

Even when we were being held by the witch and she was begging for help.'

'I take it he hasn't found them. So he's as useless as you,' Mavis said, getting louder. 'Ask him to look in on her brother. Or is that too much confusion? God forbid I would want to confuse you all.'

'Mavis! Language, *please*,' Fwl whispered, hoping Owain hadn't heard the reprimand.

Owain chuckled. 'She is funny, Fwl,' he said.

Fwl looked at Mavis and smiled nervously.

'What did he say?' she asked.

'Nothing,' he said, feeling his cheeks growing warm.

'Tell her what I said,' Owain ordered.

'I'd rather not,' Fwl whispered.

'You'd rather not what?' Mavis said, louder still.

'Go on, tell her. It might be good for her to hear we gods have a sense of humour,' Owain urged.

'Owain said you were ...' He took a breath. 'He said you were funny.'

'Funny? *Funny?* He's got a cheek!' Mavis marched forward and jabbed at the empty space next to Fwl. 'You lot are the *funny* ones, controlling people's lives!' she shouted.

Seren stirred in her sleep, and everyone turned to look at the source of the abrupt halt in snoring. It didn't last long.

Mavis turned back to the empty space next to Fwl. She was red in the face. 'Get out,' she growled.

Owain smirked. He turned back to Fwl, nodded and left with a loud pop.

'He's gone,' Fwl said.

'*Funny?* Damn cheek,' Mavis snapped.

'You're upset, Mavis.' Fwl held up his arms defensively. 'I think it's time for you to try and rest.'

'The sooner I expose you lot, the better,' Mavis snapped. She bent down and crawled onto her hay bed.

Fwl was worried about her health. Why couldn't she see that she'd be a lot happier if she calmed down and forgot about the system of gods? He lay on the hay, listening to Seren snoring. He couldn't fathom how she didn't wake herself up.

Fwl wondered if Owain would be able to find Seren's god. It seemed awfully strange that he couldn't locate them …

Owain appeared next to the window in his office.

'I have visited them,' Owain said.

'*Did you anger her?*' the voice asked.

'Yes. And they asked about Seren's god,' Owain said.

'*Did you see her?*' the voice asked quietly.

'Yes, she was sleeping.' Owain sounded amused.

'*Ah, I take it you heard her?*' said the voice.

Owain chuckled. 'I'm sure half of Armford heard her.'

The voice laughed quietly.

'Are you sure they'll be okay?' Owain asked. 'The Dewin are—'

'*They will be fine,*' said the voice.

End of part one...

Translations from Welsh to English.

Hiraeth – A longing for Wales and Welsh culture. Homesickness for Wales

Popeth – Everything

Du – Black

Glas – Blue

Melyn – Yellow

Gwyn – White

Cariad – Love

Aderyn – Bird

Printed in Great Britain
by Amazon